SHANNON'S LAW

SHANNON'S LAW

•

Charles E. Friend

AVALON BOOKS
NEW YORK

PRINTED IN THE UNITED STATES OF AMERICA
ON ACID-FREE PAPER
BY HADDON CRAFTSMEN, BLOOMSBURG, PENNSYLVANIA

This book is dedicated to my daughter, Victoria Friend Broyles, an excellent author in her own right, with special thanks to her for her help in completing this story.

Chapter One

The flat crack of a rifle shattered the afternoon silence. Clay Shannon reined up, listening intently as the sound echoed among the cliffs. A hundred yards in front of him, the trail crested and curved downward out of his line of sight. The gunshots had come from somewhere close around the bend.

Quickly, he swung the big buckskin stallion into the shelter of the boulders beside the trail. As Shannon scanned the broken slopes ahead, the horse stood with ears pricked, trembling with excitement as the last rumble of gunfire died away.

"Steady, old son," Shannon said softly. "Whoever it is, they're not shooting at us . . . yet." Still watching the trail, he reached down and slipped the rawhide thong off the hammer of his Colt and eased the Winchester in its saddle scabbard to make certain that it was free. Then he waited.

The minutes dragged by in uneasy silence. A hot trickle of sweat ran down Shannon's face from beneath his hatband. He ignored it. Eventually the horse grew restless with the heat and the inactivity; Shannon calmed the animal, holding it well back in the shelter of the boulders while he studied the rimrock. The old wound in his left knee had begun to ache after too many hours in the saddle, and he rubbed it absent-mindedly as he sat astride the buckskin, watching and listening. In that part of the country, men who rushed blindly into the unknown had a tendency to die suddenly; Shannon knew this, and the knowledge had made him careful.

At length his patience was rewarded; there was a sudden sound of hoofbeats from beyond the hill—two horses moving rapidly, their shod hooves clattering noisily over the rocky ground. Shannon slid the Winchester smoothly out of the saddle scabbard and cocked it, bracing himself for battle. Then, after a few tense moments, he relaxed. The horsemen were headed away from him, down the unseen trail on the far side of the crest. The sound faded gradually until at last the riders passed beyond hearing.

When all was quiet again, Shannon started cautiously up the hill, holding the buckskin to a slow walk as he strained his senses for any hint of danger. The harsh sunlight nearly blinded him as he scanned the tops of the cliffs ahead, and he had to put up his hand to shield his eyes from the glare. A buzzard drifted slowly into view, black against the yellow sky. The bird began to circle lazily a hundred feet above the rimrock, as if it too were waiting.

At the top of the rise Shannon paused. The trail before him curved sharply down through a defile which continued for a few hundred feet between two steep and weathered cliffs, then widened out into a small canyon. In the middle of this open area, a saddled mule was standing quietly with its reins dragging. Near the mule a set of saddlebags lay upon the ground, their meager contents strewn across the trail.

A few feet away, a man lay sprawled face down in the dust, unmoving.

Shannon swore quietly and nudged his mount forward. As he rode, his eyes moved restlessly among the rocks and along the canyon rim. In that defile he would be an easy target for anyone hidden nearby. A dislodged pebble, a startled lizard, a momentary glint of sunlight on steel—any of these might signal a bullet's imminent arrival. But there was nothing to see except the rocks, and no sound to be heard except the wind. The threat, whatever it was, had gone.

He halted a few feet from the mule and, after one last glance up at the canyon walls, dismounted stiffly, his muscles protesting. Still holding the buckskin's reins, he limped over and knelt down in the dust beside the fallen rider. The man was dead. Three bullet holes grouped closely in the center of his back told that part of the tale. There was little blood—death had come instantly.

Gently, Shannon rolled the body over. The dead man was thin and elderly; his clothing was of the type favored by the miners of the region. His glazed eyes stared sightlessly at the sky, as if watching the circling vulture. Shannon noted without surprise that the pockets of his shirt and trousers had been ripped open.

"Bushwacked and robbed," Shannon muttered to himself. The man had probably been one of the placer miners from the hills on the other side of Whiskey Creek. Looking closely, Shannon saw that on the torn cloth of the miner's left shirt pocket there was a trace of metallic yellow powder. Shannon touched the bright smear, and saw that several of the glittering particles clung to his fingertips. He rubbed them lightly between his fingers, then nodded absently to himself. Gold. The man had been leaving the gold fields, perhaps headed homeward after many months of labor, carrying a poke of gold dust. But someone else would be spending the old man's hard-earned riches now.

Shannon rose to his feet and began to examine the surrounding ground for any indication of the identity of the killers, but there was little to see on the rocky, hard-baked surface. At last, in the boulders fifty feet down the trail, he found the hoofprints of two horses. Nearby, three newly-fired rifle shells lay shining in the dust.

He inspected the tracks closely, following them a short distance down the trail. The prints were fresh, but the hard ground revealed little about either the horses or the men who had ridden them. Even to the eyes of an experienced tracker, there was nothing to distinguish these hoofprints from those of a thousand other horses that had passed along the same road.

Walking slowly back to the rocks, he retrieved the three spent cartridge casings and examined them carefully. Like the hoofprints, the shells were unremarkable—forty-four-forties, the type used by virtually everyone in that part of the country. The 1873 Winchester rifle fired these shells, as did the Colt Frontier revolver. So many men in the region carried one or both of these weapons that shell casings of that caliber would be of little use in identifying the killers. Another man might not have bothered with them, but Shannon knew from hard experience that one could never tell what might prove to be of value later. He wrapped the shells in his handkerchief and slipped them into his saddlebags.

He continued to search the area, reluctant to leave until he was sure that he had left nothing of importance undiscovered. Finally, satisfied that there was no more to be learned, he moved back up the trail to the ambush site. After tethering the mule so that it would not shy or run away, he lifted the dead miner in his arms and eased the body face down across the animal's back. He tied the corpse securely in place, took one final look around, then remounted and started down the trail leading the mule. The dead man's head bobbed grotesquely as the animal plodded along the uneven track.

Ten minutes later the trail turned again and opened out into a small valley. A mile ahead, the town of Whiskey Creek sprawled gracelessly along the meandering river that had given the settlement its name. Behind the town, a range of hills known as the Swiftwater Breaks climbed away to the north in a steadily rising jumble of steep cliffs and rocky, narrow canyons.

Shannon reined in the buckskin and sat quietly for a moment, surveying the scene. He had not been to Whiskey Creek before, but he knew its history—and its reputation. A year ago, deep in the hills above the settlement, some wandering prospector had found gold. It was not a big strike—the gold fields of California and the Dakotas were far richer—but ever since the discovery, men had been coming to pan the streams and wash away the slopes in search of yellow metal. Whiskey Creek had become the jumping-off point for the gold camp, the last "civilized" community encountered by the miners before they headed up into the canyons to seek their fortunes. The town provided them with the tools and provisions they needed to carry on their quest for riches. It also provided them, at varying intervals, with liquor, women, and the other base pleasures they sought to relieve the monotony of their labors in the hills.

Shannon looked back at the corpse tied facedown on the mule behind him. There was little doubt that the dead miner had been one of the fortunate few who had made a strike in the gold fields. The old man had tried to ride out of Whiskey Creek with his little fortune; perhaps he had dreamed of a triumphant return to a wife or family somewhere beyond the distant mountains. Instead, he had met a lonely death along the trail at the hands of men who cared more about gold than about human life.

That in itself was troubling enough, but to Shannon there was something else, something even more disturbing. The bushwhackers had been so confident that they had done their killing almost within sight of the town, and had then ridden boldly off down the trail toward it without even bothering to hide their tracks, not caring whether anyone knew where they had gone. The arrogance of it was stunning. The murderers believed, or knew, that they would not be pursued or sought out by the law to answer for their crime. In all likelihood they were in one of the local saloons by now, celebrating their savage act, perhaps even boasting about it.

Shannon felt a sudden rush of anger. Mining towns

were always rough and violent places, but the callous arrogance of these killers confirmed what Shannon already suspected—that Whiskey Creek was a lawless place where such things could and did happen, and no one cared, or dared, to do anything about it.

Until now, he thought grimly. Until now.

His jaw tightened, and something very close to hatred stirred in his soul. Clay Shannon lived in a hard world, a world governed by a few harsh and elemental principles. To him life's equation was very simple: Lawlessness is evil; decent men must fight against it; therefore, because he was a decent man, he too must fight against it. He had done so all his adult life.

And now he must do so again.

Slowly he reached into his shirt pocket, took out a nickel-plated deputy's star, and pinned it in plain sight above the left pocket of his shirt. He looked down at the shining badge to make certain that it was on straight, and then stared for a moment with narrowed eyes at the town which lay before him, the town that he had already begun to despise.

"All right, Whiskey Creek," he whispered, "ready or not, here I come."

Then he set out down the trail toward his destination, the mule plodding patiently behind him with its silent burden.

Chapter Two

Shannon rode slowly up the narrow main street of Whiskey Creek. The town was larger than he had expected: two side streets flanked the one along which he was riding, and there were several cross streets. These dusty thoroughfares, like the town itself, began along the creek and then climbed steeply up the slopes of the first low hills. High above the street, weathered sheds and dilapidated houses perched precariously on the hillsides, and Shannon found himself wondering idly if any of these structures ever broke loose and came sliding down into the town below.

The buildings he rode past were typical of that part of the country—unpainted board walls, false fronts, a few with two stories but most with only one. Many of the buildings stood alone, separated from the structures on either side by alleys or open spaces, as if the occupants did not want to be too closely associated with their neighbors. As indeed, they did not—the ever-present danger of fire in a city of wooden build-

9

ings made separation a wise precaution. There were houses and stores, saloons and smithies, boarding-houses and brothels—all of the enterprises one would expect in a community of its size, especially one that served the robust needs of a nearby mining camp. Boardwalks ran along the front walls of most of the buildings, which Shannon guessed would be sorely needed in wet weather when these hard-baked streets would undoubtedly become a sea of mud.

At first he saw few signs of life in Whiskey Creek, but as he rode along the street a few people began to come out of the stores and saloons to stare at him and at the body strapped across the back of the mule. As he moved through the center of the town he saw ahead, on his right, a large building that caught his eye immediately. It was not only larger but also more ornate than any of its neighbors. It was painted a bright yellow, and across the false front the words "Lucky Lady Saloon" had been emblazoned in curli-cued red letters several feet high. It was not just the gaudiness of the building, but something else that at-tracted Shannon's attention, something about the place that made him vaguely uneasy. Inside, a piano was playing, its tinny notes almost drowned out by peri-odic bursts of raucous laughter. For a moment, looking at the building and hearing the noises from within it, Shannon fancied that he felt a sudden coldness in the pit of his stomach. He brushed the thought aside immediately, irritated at himself. After all, one saloon was much like another. He had seen a thousand of them over the years, and there was no reason why he should be uneasy about this saloon in particular. None whatsoever.

As Shannon approached, a man lounging in a chair on the boardwalk in front of the saloon peered curiously at him, then jumped up and ran inside shouting something. Presently men began pouring out through the swinging doors, some with glasses or cards still in their hands. They stared at Shannon, pointing and exclaiming. As he passed, they began to follow him, and soon he had a growing mob of curious onlookers trailing behind him along the street. Several people shouted at him as he rode by.

"You shoot him yourself, Sheriff?" called one.

Another man yelled, "Hey, Sheriff, watch out he don't get up and run away!"

Shannon pointedly ignored them all, yet beneath his outward calm his senses had come to full alert. The crowd's hostility was not unexpected; lawmen were seldom welcome in mining towns. But there was something unusual in this animosity, a special virulence that warned Shannon to beware. Any of these people could have had a hand in the killing of the old prospector. In any case, odds were that at least one member of the crowd trailing him would be happy to shoot him in the back—with or without a reason. He moved slowly, warily, half-listening to their jeers, being careful not to provoke trouble by displaying anger or making any quick motions. "Welcome to Whiskey Creek," he thought to himself bitterly.

A hundred yards past the Lucky Lady he saw what he was looking for—a faded sign that said "Sheriff's Office." He swung the buckskin over and dismounted stiffly. As Shannon tied both horse and mule to the hitch rail at the edge of the covered boardwalk, the curiosity-seekers gathered around him, exclaiming and gesturing as they stared at the corpse and at the star on Shannon's shirt. Just as Shannon finished tying up the mule, a tall, muscular man in miner's clothing pushed through the crowd and stooped beside the mule to peer at the dead man's face.

"Know him?" said Shannon.

"Yeah," the miner said, straightening up. "It's old Joe Grubbs. Rode out of the gold camp this morning. Sold his claim a few days ago and set out for home with his stake." He shook his head. "Poor Joe. Where'd you find him?"

"On the trail about two miles south of here, up in the hills. Drygulched. Dead when I got there."

The big miner's eyes flicked down to the badge and then back to Shannon's face.

"And who might you be?" he said suspiciously.

Shannon raised his voice so that the rest of the onlookers could hear him.

"Name's Clay Shannon," he said loudly, watching their faces. "Deputy sheriff for this county."

The onlookers muttered in surprise.

"A new deputy," said someone. "Wonder how long this one will stay around?"

"We ain't had no deputy here since the last one— Watson—got killed," said the tall miner. "You come to take his place?"

"Watkins," said Shannon evenly. "His name was Watkins. Yes, I'm replacing him. Sheriff Hollister sent me down from the county seat to re-open the office."

As he spoke, a man who had been standing at the back of the crowd turned and hurried away up the street toward the Lucky Lady. Shannon watched him for a few seconds, then looked around at the remaining spectators.

"You got an undertaker here?" he asked.

The big miner shook his head.

"Naw," he said, "we got nothin' in this town but trouble. The barber usually does the buryin', but he charges too much and anyway he's always dead drunk by this time of day. If it's all the same to you, we'll take Joe up to the diggings and plant him there." He spat on the ground. "He deserves a better hole than Whiskey Creek."

"All right with me," said Shannon. He untied the mule and tossed the reins to the miner. The big man turned to two other miners who were standing near the front of the crowd.

"Shorty, how about you and Dave takin' old Joe back to the camp?" he said. Grim-faced, the two men moved forward and led the mule away. The big miner nodded morosely to Shannon, then turned to follow the others who were moving slowly away with Old Joe and his mule.

With the main attraction gone, the crowd began to disperse. Shannon could hear them talking to each other in low tones as they drifted off. He noted with wry amusement that none of them stayed to introduce themselves or talk to him, and that more than one of them turned to glance unsmilingly back over their shoulders at him as they walked away. "Friendly place," he said to his horse. "I'll bet we're really going to like it here."

He stepped up onto the boardwalk and moved to the door of the office. Both door and windows had been boarded up by someone who obviously thought that the office would not be used again for a long time. Shannon wrenched the boards away from the door-frame and then tried the door. It opened on loudly protesting hinges, and he went in.

The sunlight coming through the doorway dimly re-vealed a small room furnished only with a desk, a wooden chair, and a bunk set in one corner. The place smelled of dust and dead flies. Even with the door

open, most of the room was still in semi-darkness—
the boards nailed over the windows blocked out the
sun, turning the office into a shadowy cave. A soot-
smeared oil lamp stood on the desk; Shannon lit it and
surveyed the room. Wanted posters lay scattered like
dried leaves across the old desk and the bare wooden
floor surrounding it. A rack on the wall held two dusty
shotguns secured by a rusty chain and padlock. At the
back of the office, a heavy door set in the brick wall
opened into a jail. Two tiny cells with bunks occupied
one side of the jail area, while another bunk stood
against the opposite wall, presumably for the jailer to
use, when or if there was a jailer. There was no back
door. It was not much of a place in which to live and
work, but Shannon had been a lawman for a long time,
and he had anticipated nothing better.

He went back outside, carefully surveyed the now-
empty street, then untied the buckskin and led him
down the wide alley that ran beside the jail. Behind
the jail there was a corral large enough for two or three
horses; next to the corral was a small stable. Both had
been erected by the county years before for the use of
county employees. Shannon unsaddled the stallion and
led him into one of the stalls, brought water from the
pump behind the jail, and tossed some hay into the
manger. He took some grain from his saddlebags and
fed it to the horse. Then, carrying the saddlebags slung

over his shoulder, he walked back up the alley and re-entered the office.

The flickering light, the smoke, and the shadows cast by the oil lamp emphasized the inhospitable atmosphere of the room. Still, thought Shannon, as bad as it was, this semi-dungeon radiated warmth and charm compared with what he had so far seen of the rest of the town.

He sat down on the edge of the bunk, rubbing his knee as he looked around him. The dingy office was much like all the others of its kind he had known over the years. Too many years, he thought; too many places like this: gloomy, dirty, and depressing. That was the price of wearing a star; the price of hating evil; the price of trying to fight it. For a moment Shannon felt the loneliness pressing in upon him, the loneliness that comes to all those who venture friendless into strange and hostile lands. He had felt it before, and he knew that he would undoubtedly feel it again. It was a part of the personal cost of his chosen profession. To be alone—always.

He shook off the thought and stood up, his jaw once more set firmly. This was no time to sit around feeling sorry for himself. He had accepted this job, taken his oath, and received his star. If he had made a mistake in doing so, it was far too late to worry about it now. He had given Sheriff Hollister his word that he would enforce the law in Whiskey Creek to the best of his ability, and he would keep his word as best he could. He knew no other way.

Unbuckling his gunbelt, he hung it on a peg near the head of the bunk. He went outside and ripped the boards off the windows, then came back in and opened the shutters. The late afternoon sunlight streamed in, brightening the room. A broom lay propped in one corner; he seized it and began methodically to sweep up the dirt and dead insects which littered the floor. Presently he began to hum an old tune he had learned long ago, when he was young.

When the office was tolerably clean he put away the broom, rebuckled the gunbelt around his waist, and sat down at the desk to examine its contents. The top drawer yielded more old wanted posters decorated with a sprinkling of dead cockroaches. Beneath the pile of desiccated carcasses he found the keys to the gun rack. In the other drawers he found the key to the office door, some blank official forms, a half-empty whiskey bottle, and what appeared to be an account ledger. Shannon pocketed the keys and returned the rest of the items to their respective drawers. Then he briefly searched the rest of the office. Finding nothing of interest, he went back into the jail. The place was virtually bare. It lacked any semblance of comfort, or even the basic necessities. Among the deficiencies he found, two were especially serious—there were no blankets for the bunks and no shells for the shotguns.

Charles E. Friend

He locked the office and walked up the street, crossing to the far walk as he went. The people he passed did not greet him or meet his eye, but it did not escape his notice that when he had gone by they turned to look at him, whispering to one another. He had not expected a warm reception, even from the "decent" citizens of Whiskey Creek, and obviously he was not going to receive one.

As he came abreast of the Lucky Lady Saloon, two men walked out of the building and stood together on the covered boardwalk. They eyed him with interest as he passed by on the opposite side of the street. One of them was the man he had seen leaving the crowd that had gathered when he rode in; the other was taller and heavier, a barrel-chested man with coarse features and bushy hair. This latter individual was wearing a black frock coat over a brocaded vest, and tied beneath his boiled white collar was a flowered silk cravat— fancy dress by the standards of Whiskey Creek.

The heavy man nodded at something the other said, lit a cigar, and then gazed keenly across at Shannon. The deputy felt the man's eyes boring into his back all the way up the street. Shannon did not condescend to look back, but the cold feeling was there again in the pit of his stomach, like a prophecy. He felt certain that he would be meeting the bushy-haired watcher again.

The door creaked as Shannon entered the general

store. A man wearing a white apron greeted him from behind the counter.

"Howdy," said the storekeeper, wiping his hands on his apron. "What can I do fer ya?"

"Just came to get some supplies," Shannon said.

"Cash or credit?" asked the storekeeper suspiciously.

"Cash."

"You need anything in particular, just let me know," the man said, beaming.

Shannon picked up a pair of blankets from one of the shelves, then added a pound of coffee, a towel, and a bar of soap and placed them all on the counter. Two boxes of shotgun shells and two boxes of revolver cartridges completed his list.

"You're the new sheriff, ain't you?" said the storekeeper, shoving the cartridge boxes across the counter to him.

"Deputy sheriff. Name's Clay Shannon."

"I'm Elijah Ford. It's good to see a lawman around here again, Mr. Shannon. Maybe some of the shine on that badge will rub off on the rest of the town."

Shannon allowed himself a smile.

"It's my job to see that it does," he said. One person, at least, was glad to see him. It was a start.

He was paying for his purchases when the door slammed open and a bearded man of huge size staggered into the store. He was dressed in mud-spattered clothes, and in one huge paw he was carrying a broken shovel. Even before Shannon smelled the whiskey on his breath he could see that the man was drunk.

Ignoring Shannon, the miner swayed unsteadily up to the counter and slammed the shovel down in front of the storekeeper.

"Here, you bandy-legged little runt," he roared, "this shovel you sold me ain't no good. Busted the first time I tried to use it. I want a new shovel or else gimme my money back."

Elijah Ford examined the shovel. "Looks to me like you tried to pry on something with this," he said. "A shovel ain't meant to be used as a crowbar, you know."

"Don't play games with me, mister," cried the miner. "That shovel's no good." He reached across the counter and grabbed the storekeeper by the shirtfront. "Now, are you gonna gimme my money back or do I have to break you into little pieces?"

"That's enough, friend," Shannon said mildly. The miner released Ford and turned to glare at Shannon.

"Who asked you to stick your nose in my business?" he growled, his fists bunching at his side.

"This is the new sheriff," said the storekeeper, backing away from the counter. "Just got into town today."

The miner blinked, noticing for the first time the badge on Shannon's shirt.

"Well, so he is," the miner said. "Another tin star.

Bet he don't last no longer than the other one." His attention returned to the shovel. "What about my money?"

"Come back tomorrow when you're sober," Shannon suggested. "You can settle it then."

"Look out, Sheriff," the storekeeper cried nervously. "He's a rough 'un. I've had trouble with him before. He'll probably try to knife you."

"Aw," the miner said disgustedly, "I ain't gonna hurt him." He laughed loudly. "The boys in the Lucky Lady will take care of that soon enough, I reckon." He jabbed his finger at Shannon's chest. "All right, Mr. Law, I don't want no trouble with you. I ain't *that* drunk. I'll come back tomorrow. Right now I think I'll go get me another whiskey." He headed unsteadily toward the door, the broken shovel already forgotten.

"See ya at the funeral, Sheriff," he called as he went out. "Yours, that is!" He disappeared down the boardwalk, guffawing at his own wit.

"What did he mean about the Lucky Lady?" Shannon said to the storekeeper. The man's previously friendly manner disappeared, and he averted his eyes from Shannon's gaze. His adam's apple began to bob nervously up and down, and he shook his head emphatically.

"T-t-this ain't my affair," he said. "Go ask somebody else."

Shannon picked up his purchases.

"Thanks," he said wryly.

An hour later he was sitting at his desk looking through some old papers he had found on a shelf in the jail. The sun was setting, and he had just closed the shutters and turned up the wick of the oil lamp when he heard a soft footfall on the boardwalk outside the office. He placed the papers quietly on the desk and rose from the chair, easing his Colt Peacemaker silently out of its oiled holster. He blew out the lamp and crouched at the end of the desk, waiting. When it came, the soft knock on the door seemed loud in the stillness.

"Come in if you're peaceful," Shannon said evenly.

The door swung slowly open and a man stood in the doorway, silhouetted against the twilight. He peered uncertainly into the darkened office, trying to locate its occupant. Shannon cocked the six-gun very deliberately, letting the other man hear the sound. The visitor snickered and carefully lifted his hands so that they rested in plain sight on the sides of the door frame.

"What's the matter, Deputy?" he said. "Nervous?" Although the man's face was not visible, the sneer was apparent in the voice.

Holding the Colt ready, Shannon relit the lamp and examined his visitor. The stranger was of above medium height, heavily built, dressed in a black suit. His face was fleshy and pockmarked, and there was no humor in the dark, glittering eyes. Beneath the suit coat were two heavy revolvers in black holsters, and the holsters were tied down. This character's no miner, Shannon thought drily, recognizing the man for what he was. Shannon had met many gunfighters, and had liked very few of them. He knew instinctively that this was one he would not like.

He put the lamp down and sat on the edge of the desk, resting the cocked six-gun ostentatiously across his lap. The visitor laughed, a flat, mirthless, ugly sound.

"Relax," he said. "I'm just bringin' you a message. Friendly, like."

"Have we met?" Shannon said.

"Name's Slade. Nick Slade. Maybe you heard of me?"

"Can't say I have," said Shannon, yawning. Annoyance flashed across the gunman's face.

"I'm a friend of Ace Parker."

"Who's Ace Parker?"

"You *are* a babe in the woods, ain't you? Well, you'll find out soon enough who Ace Parker is. He owns the Lucky Lady and a lot of other things around here."

"Including you?"

Slade straightened up, his face suddenly flushed.

"Don't push me, friend," he snarled. "It ain't healthy, as more than one man has found out."

Shannon nodded affably.

"I'll try to remember that. You said you had a message for me?"

"Mr. Parker wants to meet you."

"Delighted. I'll be here whenever he wants to drop in."

"Mr. Parker wants you to come up to the Lucky Lady. He likes to do all of his business there. He says maybe you could stop by later this evening."

Shannon gently uncocked the six-gun and returned it to the holster.

"Maybe," he said. "Maybe not. Anything else?"

Slade looked coldly at him for a few seconds, then shrugged.

"Your choice. Might be worth your while, though, since you're goin' to be the new deputy here."

"How did Mr. Parker get along with the old deputy?"

Slade's eyes narrowed. "Watkins? He's dead."

"I know," said Shannon. "Where were you when it happened?"

Slade's face paled, and he stared at Shannon for a moment with naked dislike. Then he laughed again.

"You live dangerously, mister," he said. "Well, let me give you a piece of neighborly advice. You'd better walk a little softer until you get to know what's what around here. That way you'll live longer." He turned on his heel and vanished into the gathering darkness.

Shannon moved to the door and watched Slade walk up the boardwalk toward the Lucky Lady. The gunman passed through the yellow squares of light thrown onto the walk by the windows of the saloon and disappeared between the swinging doors.

Shannon leaned against the doorframe, letting the tension ease out of his body. He had never heard of Slade by name, but he knew the type well—far too well. There were men like him in every untamed town in the West: men with fast guns and few morals, men easy to hire—the kind who put notches on the handles of their six-guns and brag about not counting Mexicans and Indians. Such men could be dangerous enemies, and clearly he and Slade were going to be enemies. He had obviously touched a nerve when he asked Slade about the dead deputy, Watkins. One way or another, he and Slade would almost certainly meet again, perhaps soon.

He glanced casually up and down the street. It was now full dark, and the alleys and doorways along the dusty road lay deep in shadow. He could see no one, but a hundred men could be hiding out there, waiting for him. Waiting armed, and perhaps filled with malice. The thought was not exactly comforting.

As he stood contemplating the street, Shannon suddenly became aware of a delicious aroma drifting on the night air. Somewhere, someone was cooking steak. He looked around and discovered the source of the odor immediately—directly across from the office was a small restaurant. The sign on the door said "Swiftwater Café." Beyond its brightly lit front window he could see a woman in a blue dress moving about, placing silverware on the tables. It struck him suddenly that he had eaten nothing since early morning, and that he was ravenously hungry. He fished the door key out of his pocket, locked the office, and followed the aroma across the street.

Chapter Three

A spring-mounted bell tinkled merrily as he pushed open the curtained front door of the restaurant. There were no customers in the place, but the bell's peal brought the woman in the blue dress out of the kitchen. Squinting a little in the unaccustomed light, Shannon saw that she was tall and slightly younger than he was—late twenties, perhaps. Her hair was blonde, and her eyes, he noted, were startlingly blue. He could not help but also notice that she was attractive and gracefully proportioned, but he carefully put the thought aside.

"Evening, ma'am," he said. "Your cooking smelled so good from across the way that I thought I'd come over and see what it tasted like. Any chance of getting a steak and some coffee?"

The woman laughed—a nice laugh, Shannon thought—and picked up a menu from the counter.

"Good evening, Deputy," she said. "That smell is the only advertising I can afford, so I'm glad it worked. Come on in. Where would you like to sit?"

He chose the table farthest from the door and slid into the chair next to the wall so he could watch the door as he ate. The woman placed the menu before him and then poured him a steaming cup of coffee from a large pot.

"I'm Kathy Winters," she said, offering her hand to him.

"Clay Shannon," he replied as they shook hands.

"I know. You've been sent down from the county seat to be the town's new sheriff."

"Deputy sheriff. News travels fast around this town."

"There aren't many secrets here, believe me. I'm glad you're here. Whiskey Creek needs all the law it can get." She sighed, then smiled warmly. "Now, how would you like your steak?"

He gave her his order. She hurried into the kitchen, and he could hear her moving around, clattering utensils as she prepared the meal. Presently she began to sing quietly as she went about her work. It was a good sound, a sound not often heard in Shannon's world, and he listened with growing pleasure as he drank his coffee. In a few minutes she was back with a huge portion of beef sizzling on a hot iron plate. He nodded his thanks as she placed it before him.

"Mighty good coffee, ma'am," he said. "Wish I could make it like that."

She smiled, pleased by the compliment. He picked

up his knife and fork, expecting her to turn away and resume her work. Instead she remained beside the table, hesitating as if wanting to say something and not knowing how to put it.

"What is it, ma'am?" he said, cutting into the steak.

She sat down on the edge of the table's other chair, smoothed her white apron, and looked searchingly at him.

"Do you know much about this town, Mr. Shannon?" she said at last.

"Enough to know that not many people here are going to be glad to see me."

"The other deputy—the one who was killed. Was he a friend of yours?"

Shannon shook his head as he chewed.

"Never met him. I was sworn in after he was already dead."

"Are you here to find out who murdered him?"

"That's part of it, yes ma'am. It seems a lot of people have been getting killed around here. Like the old man I found on the trail today."

"There've been others, you know. Many others." She looked down at her feet and then back at him. "My husband was one of them."

Shannon put down his fork, taken aback.

"I'm sorry," he said lamely. "I didn't know. Was he . . . are you from around these parts originally?"

"No. We had a general store in St. Louis. A year

ago, Bob—that was my husband—sold the store to come up here to the gold fields. He promised to send for me in a few months, and he did. I came as soon as I heard from him. When I got off the stage here in town they told me that he had been killed just the night before. He was ambushed on the road coming down from the gold camp to meet me. He's buried in the cemetery outside of town."

"They find out who did it?"

"Nobody even *tried* to find out who did it. Mr. Watkins wasn't here then, and the sheriff's office had been closed for a long time. Shootings are common around here, and no one in this town cared enough about Bob's death even to ask questions about it. No one except me, and nobody would talk to me or tell me anything." She turned her head away, but Shannon saw that there were tears in her eyes.

She gave a slight gesture of impatience.

"I didn't mean to get into all that," she said. "What I wanted to say to you, what I wanted to warn you about, was. . . . Mr. Shannon, please be careful. This is a rotten town, and there are some rotten people in it. A lot of good men have died here. Don't let them get you too."

Shannon shifted uncomfortably in his chair. He wasn't used to having anyone care what happened to him, especially a stranger, and it disturbed him a little.

"I'm not so easy to kill," he said, forcing a grin.

This made her tears well up even further, but she said nothing. Shannon tried to think of something to say to end the awkward silence.

"What can you tell me about this man Parker who owns the Lucky Lady Saloon?" he said, watching her.

"Be especially careful of him, Mr. Shannon," she said. "He runs this town—most of it, anyway. He's a ruthless thug who hires others to do his dirty work for him." She hesitated a moment, then continued. "Perhaps it's only a coincidence, but quite a few of the people who've been killed died very soon after leaving the Lucky Lady."

"Thank you for the warning," Shannon said. For some reason, he did not find the information particularly surprising.

The door of the restaurant opened and an elderly couple came in. They called a greeting to Mrs. Winters and seated themselves at a table by the window.

Kathy Winters stood up, wiping her hands on her apron.

"I have to get back to work now," she said. "Is the steak all right?"

"Best I've ever tasted," he replied truthfully. "You open for breakfast, by any chance?"

She was cheerful again now.

"Six A.M. sharp," she said. "Best flapjacks in town."

"I'll be here."

She gave him another searching look.

"I hope so," she said uneasily. Then her smile returned. "See you in the morning, then." She moved away to deliver menus to the other table.

Shannon stood on the boardwalk outside the restaurant, thinking about what the woman had told him. The night was warm but not uncomfortably so. From one of the saloons up the street came the sound of a piano playing an off-key version of a popular drinking song. He heard voices, and saw that several men were coming out of the swinging doors of the Lucky Lady. They stumbled away, laughing.

He looked across at the office. Through the chinks in the shutters he could see the glow of the oil lamp which he had left burning on the desk. Shannon stretched his arms and then rubbed his aching back. It had been a long day, and he was very tired. He thought of the bunk in the office; the prospect of sleep was inviting.

"Getting too old for this job, I guess," he muttered. He turned and strode firmly up the street toward the Lucky Lady Saloon. Sleep would have to wait.

He pushed cautiously through the swinging doors of the Lucky Lady and glanced around him. The room was larger than he had anticipated, and displayed an elegance he would not have expected to find in a dirty, ramshackle place like Whiskey Creek. A mahogany bar ran along one side of the room, and a large plate glass mirror adorned the wall behind the bar. The room was brightly lit; three ornate brass oil lamps hung from the low beams of the ceiling, and several smaller lamps were spaced at intervals around the walls. By their light Shannon saw that much of the floor space was occupied by gaming tables—dice, roulette, blackjack, faro, poker. However, at this early hour few of the denizens of Whiskey Creek were taking advantage of the facilities. One man was bucking the roulette wheel and another was trying his hand at blackjack, but the other tables were deserted, and there was only a single drinker at the bar.

Shannon instinctively looked for a back door to the saloon, a reflex born of long experience. To a lawman, a saloon's back door could be an unobtrusive entrance, a quick means of exit, or a source of deadly danger. He quickly spotted it—at the rear of the room were two doorways, one of which stood half-open to reveal the alley that ran behind the building. A red velvet curtain blocked his view of whatever lay beyond the other door. Perhaps an office, Shannon thought, or perhaps something else. He would have to find out. As he watched, a man who had been lounging at the back of the room slipped quietly through the curtain and disappeared.

All conversation in the room had stopped when he came in. Ignoring the stares, he walked over to the bar.

"Beer," he said. The bartender glanced sullenly at the badge, then filled a glass to overflowing and slapped it down on the bar just beyond easy reach. Shannon grinned and tossed a coin over the bar into the sawdust at the bartender's feet. The bartender glowered, then reluctantly bent over and picked it up. Shannon retrieved the beer, found a table against the wall, and sank into the chair which commanded the best view of the room. He sipped the lukewarm beer, watching the play at the nearby roulette and blackjack tables. He was confident that he would not have long to wait.

Two men came through the curtained doorway at the rear. One of them was Nick Slade, the other was the frock-coated man who had been standing in front of the Lucky Lady earlier in the day as Shannon walked past. His coat, fancy vest, and silk tie seemed out of place on his burly frame. It was as if he were wearing a costume, posing as someone or something that he was not. When he reached up to remove the long black cigar from his lips, the diamond rings on his hand sparkled in the lamplight, and when he smiled it reminded Shannon of a wolf showing its teeth.

The man said something to Slade; the gunman grunted in reply and then moved unhurriedly over to the bar directly opposite Shannon's table. He leaned back against the bar, eyeing Shannon with an amused half-sneer on his face.

The man in the frock coat swaggered up to the table and stopped, his hands hooked in his lapels.

"Sheriff Shannon?"

"Deputy sheriff."

"Right, yeah. I'm Ace Parker. Thanks for coming in."

"That's all right," Shannon said. "I was thirsty anyway."

Parker frowned, pulled out a chair, and sat down across the table from Shannon, blocking his view of Slade at the bar. Shannon got up and shifted his chair slightly to one side so that he had an unobstructed view of the gunman. Parker watched this maneuver without comment. Slade's sneer became a grin.

"So," Parker said, "Sheriff Hollister sent you down to replace Watkins." It was a statement, not a question. Shannon said nothing, keeping his eyes on Slade. "We all miss poor Watkins," Parker said. "He was a good man."

He eyed the ivory-handled Colt in Shannon's holster.

"You done much of this kind of work?" he said.

"A little," Shannon said indifferently.

"Don't be so modest. As a matter of fact," Parker continued, "I heard you were carryin' a badge up in Kansas for awhile."

Shannon took a sip of beer.

"Long time ago," he said.

"Why'd you pull out and head down this way?" Parker asked, sucking on his cigar.

"That's my business."

Parker flushed slightly.

"Sure," he said, "but I'm glad you're an old hand at this. We need real lawmen in Whiskey Creek, not greenhorns. I like men who've been around, men who know the ropes. Men who know when to be, uh, reasonable."

Shannon looked at him.

"What do you mean by 'reasonable?' " he said, knowing perfectly well what Parker had meant.

"I mean that I like men who know when to keep their noses out of things. Men who don't interfere with other people too much. Men who can give a little help when it's needed." Parker leaned over so that his face was just inches away and added in a lower voice, "Men who know which side their bread's buttered on."

Incredible, thought Shannon. I've been in town less than four hours and already this overdressed tinhorn is offering me a bribe. He glanced over at Slade. The gunman was watching the proceedings with unconcealed amusement.

"Just how much 'butter' are we talking about here, Mr. Parker?" Shannon said quietly.

Parker grinned again. There was a gleam of triumph in his eyes.

"Well, I'd rather not say too much until we know

each other better, but it seems only fair that if you're going to be helping me out on your own time, so to speak, you ought to be paid for it. No reasonable man could object to that."

"What about Watkins?" Shannon said. "Was he 'reasonable'? Or is that why he wound up in lying in the dirt with a couple of slugs in his back?"

Parker's face reddened.

"We're not talking about Watkins now," he said harshly. "We're talking about you. A man in your position can become rich in no time if he knows when to take a hand and when to look the other way. You'll find I can be very generous under the right circumstances. Now what about it? Do we have a deal?"

Shannon drained the last of the beer and nonchalantly stood up.

"I'll give it some thought," he said. "In the meantime, Mr. Parker, I think you'd better do something about your gambling tables. Even from here I can see that the roulette wheel is rigged and the blackjack dealer is palming cards. If you don't clean up your games, I'm afraid I'll have to close them down."

Parker's jaw dropped in disbelief. His face reddened even further and the veins stood out on either side of his meaty neck. Slade threw back his head and laughed his mirthless laugh.

"I was right, Deputy," Slade said. "You do like to live dangerously."

"Just doing my job, gentlemen," said Shannon. "Nothing personal. Good night."

He started toward the front door, moving slowly, hoping that nobody would decide to shoot him before he reached the street. He had prodded the saloon-keeper hard, perhaps too hard for a first meeting, and on the man's own ground at that. Parker and Slade would have to be very confident indeed to backshoot him in their own saloon in front of a dozen witnesses—but they just might be that confident.

A single rivulet of sweat trickled down Shannon's back as he pushed through the swinging doors and walked, gratefully alive, out into the coolness of the evening.

Chapter Four

Shannon crossed the street from the office in the clear light of dawn and, true to his word, entered the door of Kathy Winters' restaurant at precisely 6:01 A.M. She came out of the kitchen tying her apron. It occurred vaguely to Shannon that she seemed relieved to see him.

"You're my first customer of the day," she said as he settled into the same chair he had occupied the previous evening. "Still want those flapjacks?"

"Sure do, if the offer's still open."

When she brought the laden plate to the table, he rose and pulled out one of the other chairs for her.

"Do you have time to talk a little?" he said. She hesitated for a moment and then sat down.

"I'll stay as long as I can," she said. "People will start coming in soon."

"I'm obliged," he said, taking his seat.

"I saw you going up the street toward the Lucky Lady after you left here last night," she said. "Did you see Parker?"

"Yes."

"What happened?"

"He tried to buy me."

Kathy Winters nodded.

"That's what he would do, at least at first," she said. "I'm guessing he didn't have much luck with you."

Shannon wiped his mouth with his napkin.

"I'm no better than the next man, Mrs. Winters," he said, "and I don't pretend to be. But when you carry the star you have to live up to what it stands for or you're nothing. Less than nothing, in fact. No, he didn't have any luck."

She reached over and laid her hand lightly on his.

"I think perhaps you are better than the next man, Mr. Shannon," she said. She withdrew her hand and looked down at her apron. "I hate to say it, but I think you may be better than the last one, too."

"You mean Watkins? Are you suggesting that he might have been on Parker's payroll?"

"I've heard people say so."

"Well, if he was, they must have had a falling out."

"Yes. A lot of people think Parker had him killed."

"They may be right. I mean to find out, if I can. But that isn't going to be easy." He shook his head ruefully. "Look, Mrs. Winters," he said, "the truth is that unless somebody talks, I haven't got a prayer of catching whoever killed your husband or any of the others. Any evidence there might have been is long lost now. I don't even have any clue as to who shot that old miner yesterday, and I came along just minutes after he died."

"You have no idea at all?"

"No, none. Or at least almost none. Sure, it might have been Parker's bunch. But suspicion is one thing, proof is another. Besides, Parker isn't the only wolf in these hills. There are plenty of people around here who would gladly kill a man for a lot less than old Joe Grubbs had in his poke. Still, these incidents may all be related. I'm going to start with Watkins' murder. If I can find out who killed him, I may know who killed your husband and all the rest as well."

He paused and rubbed his eyes.

"The trouble is, I'm going to need some help and I don't have any. The county seat is two days' ride and there's no telegraph. And even if I were to send for help, Sheriff Hollister doesn't have enough men to spare anybody else for Whiskey Creek just now. I'm on my own here, and I still know very little about the town, about the people here, or even about how a county deputy came to be gunned down in the middle of the street one night."

Kathy Winters folded her hands in her lap.

"I understand," she said. "How can I help?"

Shannon looked at her thoughtfully for a long moment.

"Before you decide whether or not to help me, Mrs.

Winters, you must clearly understand something. I'm a marked man here, marked already by Parker and his crowd—and maybe by some other people too—as somebody they don't want around. Anyone who helps me is taking a chance of being added to their list."

He watched her closely as he spoke. He needed her assistance, but if there was any doubt, any hesitancy on her part, he would keep her out of it.

"I'll take the chance," she said, her eyes flashing. "I have a score to settle, remember? Now, what can I do?"

Shannon felt a little of the burden lifting from his shoulders. At least there was one person in Whiskey Creek who was willing to help him, someone who eventually might be called a friend. As he looked at her he again became aware of her attractiveness, and it made him uneasy. He had work to do in this town, and until it was done there was no room for thoughts of anything else. Many a lawman had found that sort of distraction to be fatal, and Shannon had no intention of making the same mistake. He must regard this woman as a source of information, and nothing else.

"Did Watkins have any helpers?" he said. "A jailer, a swamper, anything?"

"Yes. Old Pop Bentley. He used to work for the stage line until his rheumatism got bad and they let him go. He swept out the sheriff's office for Mr. Watkins and acted as jailer when there was a prisoner."

"What about Watkins' death? All we heard up at the county seat is that he was found dead on some side street here in town one night, shot twice in the back. Where did it happen?"

"His body was discovered late one evening in the alley next to the Lucky Lady."

"Who found him—not Nick Slade by any chance?"

"No, it was Mr. Rodriguez, Pedro Rodriguez. Most people call him Pete. He works at the freight yard and sometimes rides shotgun on the stagecoach. He lives on the next street over—his house is just behind your stable. His wife helps me out in the kitchen now and then."

They talked for a few more minutes, until customers began drifting in. Then he got up, reaching into his pocket for the money to pay for the meal. Kathy Winters stood up too, and it seemed to Shannon that she was reluctant to end the conversation. It occurred to him that perhaps she was lonely too.

"Will you be in again later?" she said, retying her apron.

"Can you think of a better place to eat?" he said.

"Not in this town."

"Then I'll be back."

Pedro Rodriguez' house was, as Kathy Winters had said, immediately behind the county stable. It was a small house made of adobe, with a little yard in the rear where two young children were playing enthusiastically in the dirt. Shannon walked around to the front of the house and knocked on the frame of the open door. A short, full-bodied woman came out of the back of the house brushing flour from her hands.

"Sí, señor?" she said politely.

"Good morning, ma'am," said Shannon. "I wonder if I might speak to Mr. Rodriguez?"

"Of course, *señor*. He is in the kitchen. Will you come inside?"

"No, thank you, ma'am, I'll just wait here if you don't mind."

She disappeared, and in a few moments a stocky man dressed in worn but clean work clothes came to the door.

"Mr. Rodriguez?"

The man nodded. Shannon introduced himself.

"May I talk with you?" he said. "It's about Mr. Watkins."

Rodriguez nodded again. "Certainly. It was I who found him, as you probably already know. Please come in and sit down."

Shannon followed him into the cool interior of the house. When they were seated, Rodriguez said, "Now, how can I be of service?"

"I'd be much obliged if you could tell me about finding Mr. Watkins' body."

"There is not much to tell. I was walking home

down the main street from the freight yard. I had just finished a long haul in from the mines and it was late—perhaps a little past midnight. I heard two shots up ahead. I did not think too much of it at first, because it was Saturday night and there were many miners in town. When the miners become drunk they often fire shots into the air for no reason. But when I came past the alley that runs next to the Lucky Lady Saloon I looked down it and saw a man's body lying in the darkness. I went over to him, thinking he might just be passed out from too much whiskey, but when I lit a match I saw the wounds in his back, and when I rolled him over I realized it was Mr. Watkins."

"Did he say anything before he died?"

"No, he was already dead when I reached him."

Shannon pondered this information. It was more or less what he had expected. Watkins was not the first lawman to meet death in the dark alleys of an untamed town.

"Look, Mr. Rodriguez," he said, "do you have a few more minutes to spare? I'm sorry to have to take up any more of your time, but it might help me a great deal if you could show me exactly where this happened."

"But of course," said Rodriguez, rising. "I do not have to go to the freight yard today. I will be happy to show you if it will be of assistance." He walked over to the door, took a worn gunbelt down from a peg, and strapped it on.

"You will forgive me, I hope," he said, gesturing at the holster. "These are difficult times, and a man must be prepared."

They walked up the main street together, making small talk. Rodriguez seemed cheerful but just a little wary. When asked, he confirmed that he did indeed ride shotgun for the stage line upon occasion. Although they did not discuss it, there was something about Rodriguez' manner and the way he wore his gunbelt that suggested to Shannon that the man was comfortable with firearms and probably knew how to use them well. The walnut handles of the Smith and Wesson .44 in his holster were well-worn, yet the metal of the gun was bright and clean, and Shannon had the feeling that if he were to look closer at the weapon he would find the mechanism smooth and well-oiled.

They proceeded up the street past the Lucky Lady. A couple of loungers on the boardwalk outside the saloon eyed them as they went by. A few yards further on, Rodriguez stopped and turned.

"I was about here," he said, "walking down the hill, when I heard the shots. As I told you, I thought little of it then, and I continued walking, so." He moved back down the street toward the Lucky Lady, and Shannon followed.

"Here," Rodriguez said as he came opposite the alley, "I first saw the body." He moved down the alley and stopped at the rear corner of the saloon, a few feet from the wall. "He was lying here. He was face down, not moving."

Shannon looked around. The alley was flanked on the one side by the saloon, on the other side by what appeared to be a boardinghouse. At the end of the saloon building the alley made a ninety-degree turn to the left and ran down behind the Lucky Lady and a number of other buildings, passing eventually between the stable behind the sheriff's office and Rodriguez' back yard. It seemed to extend right on to the edge of town—an ideal escape route for an assassin.

"When you found the body, Mr. Rodriguez, was anyone else around?"

"There were a few people on the street, mostly miners coming and going from the saloon, here. No one came into the alley until I shouted for help."

"Who came then?"

"A few miners. They were all drunk, I think. Some of the people from the saloon came out too."

"Was Nick Slade there?"

"*Sí.* He came out of the Lucky Lady."

"Did he come from the front or the back of the saloon?

"From the back."

"How long after the shots?"

Rodriguez thought for a moment.

"Several minutes, I would say. Three, perhaps four. By then I had sent for the doctor." He paused, frowning a little. "One other thing. It may mean nothing, but just after the shots were fired and before I reached the alley I heard the footsteps of a man running. The sound must have come from the alley—there was no one running in the street at that time. And as I started down the alley toward Mr. Watkins' body, I think I heard a door closing somewhere back there." He gestured down the alley which ran behind the saloon. "I cannot be sure about this last part, you understand— there was some noise in the street, miners laughing and calling to one another. I could have been mistaken."

"I doubt you were mistaken," Shannon said grimly. The back door of the Lucky Lady was not twenty feet from where Watkins had died.

Rodriguez grimaced.

"I know what you are thinking, my friend," he said, "but go slowly. There are some things that are better left unsaid—at least for now."

"Yes," Shannon said. "For now." He was studying the two-story structure that stood across the alley from the Lucky Lady. A second-floor window opened directly onto the alley opposite the spot where Watkins had died.

"That place there," he said, indicating it to Rodriguez. "Is it just a boardinghouse, or . . ."

Rodriguez snorted.

"The owner calls it a boardinghouse, but most of the boarders are women who work in the Lucky Lady. They use the rooms to entertain, you understand."

Shannon was still staring at the window. It was a long chance, but still. . . .

"What's the owner's name?"

"It is *Señora* Williamson. She is a—how do you say it?—a business associate of *Señor* Parker."

"That figures," said Shannon. He looked around; two men he had never seen before had paused in the entrance to the alley and were watching curiously. When they realized that Shannon had seen them, they turned hurriedly and went across the walk and into the Lucky Lady.

"Let's head back to your place," Shannon said to Rodriguez. "I've seen enough."

They started back down the main street. Shortly after they passed the Lucky Lady, Shannon sensed someone behind them. Turning, he saw Nick Slade sauntering easily down the opposite boardwalk a few feet to their rear.

"We've got company," Shannon said to Rodriguez. "Nick Slade. He must have come out of the saloon and crossed over behind us."

Rodriguez did not turn to look.

"Slade? I do not like that one," he said. "He kills for money. And I think he is the kind of man who also kills for pleasure."

When they reached the office, Shannon turned to Rodriguez.

"Look, Mr. Rodriguez," he said, "I'm very grateful to you for your help. I hope no one makes trouble for you because of it. If you have any problem with anyone, please let me know."

Rodriguez shrugged his shoulders.

"I am glad to be able to assist you in this matter," he said. "I hope you will call upon me again if I can be of further service. As for trouble, well, I have known much of it in my life, and I have learned to take care of myself. Do not be worried because of me."

He looked across to where Slade was leaning indolently against a storefront, watching them. The dislike was plain on Rodriguez' face.

"Someday," he said, "this Nick Slade, like all gunfighters, will meet a man who is faster than himself. Who knows, *amigo*, perhaps it will be you."

He turned and walked away toward his home.

Shannon waited until he was gone and then stepped down into the street, crossing to the spot where Slade was standing.

"Was there something you wanted, Slade?" he said

as he stepped up on the walk. Slade displayed his sneering grin.

"Just out for a walk, Sheriff. No law against that, is there?"

"No," said Shannon, "but there's a law against following me around. It's a good law. I just made it up. Now, for your information, I'm going down the hill to find Pop Bentley. If you're all that interested, you can walk along with me, and we'll talk about the weather or whatever it is you want to talk about. Otherwise, stay away from me. If I see you following me again, I'll toss you in jail and let you sit there while I go about my business."

He wheeled and walked off down the street, leaving Slade standing on the walk glowering at him.

Chapter Five

Following the directions given him by Kathy Winters, Shannon found Pop Bentley's modest house at the end of the street near the creek. It was only a shack, a windowless collection of weathered boards crowned by a peeling tarpaper roof. A dilapidated wooden pen populated by four pigs stood close to the house. The old man himself was sitting in a rickety chair tilted back against his front wall, peeling potatoes.

"Howdy," he said. "Wondered when you'd get around to me." He waved at another chair nearby. "Sit a spell if you're a-minded." Shannon took the offered chair. He looked back up the street, but there was no sign of Slade, so he turned to the older man.

"I hear you took care of the jail for Watkins. I was wondering if you'd be interested in doing the same for me."

"Sure you want me?" Bentley asked. "Accordin' to everybody else around here, I ain't much good for anythin' anymore. Got the rheumatiz, ya know."

"I want you," Shannon said. "County pay scale—dollar a day, starting right now. When I have prisoners you stay in the jail during the day and sleep there at night. Otherwise you can come and go as you please once the place is cleaned up."

"Have to come down here a couple of times a day to look after my hogs. That okay?"

"Fine with me. What do you say?"

Bentley rubbed the grey stubble on his face.

"Beats peelin' taters," he said. "You got any prisoners up there now? Haven't heard of you arrestin' anybody."

"Not yet," said Shannon, "but the office needs swamping out, and it may not be very long before we'll have some boarders. Can you come up later today?"

"Sure. Gimme a few minutes to collect some stuff, and I'll be along." He chuckled. "Just like old times," he said. "Can't wait until you arrest somebody!"

The old man was as good as his word. Within the hour he was in the office and hard at work sweeping up, opening the windows, and airing the bunk mattresses. While Bentley worked, Shannon sat in a chair outside the office door thumbing through Watkins' ledger. All of the entries were routine, relating mostly to expenses incurred in running the office. There was nothing to suggest payoffs from Parker or any other impropriety, and Shannon was glad. Watkins was dead, and there was no point in fouling his name now. He had died wearing the star, and until someone proved otherwise Shannon preferred to assume he had died wearing it honorably. Besides, whether he had been honest or not, the man had been murdered, and his murderers must be found.

Shannon was about to get up and put the ledger back in the desk when he heard running feet echoing along the boardwalk. He looked up and saw the surly bartender from the Lucky Lady hurrying toward him.

"Hey, Sheriff," the man called. "Come quick!"

"What's the matter?" Shannon said, leaning back in the chair.

"Got one of them cussed miners in the Lucky Lady," puffed the bartender. "Drunker than a hoot owl, and makin' trouble. Mr. Parker said to fetch you right away."

Shannon stared at the man, warning bells ringing in his brain. Ace Parker's toughs were more than capable of handling one drunken miner, however large or well-armed he might be. They would have dealt with such situations hundreds of times in the past without help from the law. If there really was a drunk making trouble in the saloon, this could be some kind of a test. Perhaps Parker and Slade wanted to see how he would handle himself. Or perhaps there was no drunk, and this was a trap. More than one lawman had been lured to his death in just this manner. Either way, he decided, he'd have to go—he couldn't just sit there and do nothing. If he did, they'd say he was yellow. He'd be laughed out of town. Out of the county, perhaps.

Pop Bentley emerged from the office.

"Whatcha gonna do, son?" he said.

Shannon stood up. "My job, I guess."

The old man directed a stream of tobacco juice into the street.

"Could be a stacked deck," he said. "Better not go."

Shannon smiled grimly. "I wish I didn't have to, Pop," he said, checking the cylinder of his Colt.

The Lucky Lady seemed cool and dark after the glare of the street. Shannon paused just inside the swinging doors, letting his eyes adjust. There were a dozen men in the saloon, and Shannon recognized most of them as Parker's own people. They were standing well away from the bar, backed up around the walls in a rough semi-circle. Another man, a miner by his appearance, was sitting at a back table holding a bloody bar towel to his head. Parker himself was standing near the center of the room, resplendent in his frock coat. He was chewing viciously on his habitual cigar. Slade stood a few feet beyond him, his eyes fastened unwaveringly on Shannon. The bar itself was empty except for one man, a broad-shouldered, bearded miner who was standing unsteadily with his foot on the brass rail, banging an empty whiskey glass on the top of the bar. The broken pieces of a shattered bottle were spread out across the bar and on the floor around the miner's feet.

"Whiskey, I said! I want some whiskey!" he bellowed. "Where's that fool bartender? I want some service here!"

Shannon regarded the shouting miner with a professional eye. The man was of average height but solidly built, drunk enough to be belligerent but not too drunk to put up a fight. And he was wearing a gun, an old Remington percussion revolver by the look of it, jammed down into a soft leather holster. Shannon could guess that even if the miner knew how to use the gun properly, which was doubtful, his draw would be slow. Nick Slade must know that too. Slade could have subdued or killed the man easily, if he had wanted—or been ordered—to do so. Shannon realized that he had been right; this was either a test or a trap, and he had walked into it.

"Having a problem, Mr. Parker?" he said.

"Glad you're here, Sheriff," Parker said, waving his cigar. "That idiot at the bar wants to fight everybody in the place." He jerked a thumb at the injured man sitting at the rear table. "Broke a bottle over his own sidekick's head, and wants to take everybody else on too."

"And your own people couldn't handle him?"

Parker smirked.

"That's what you get paid for, ain't it? This is one tough *hombre*. He's armed, he's disturbing the peace, he's busting up private property, and he's hurting people. You're the sheriff. Now, what are you gonna do about it?"

Shannon sighed and walked up to the bar. The miner, startled by his approach, whirled to face him.

"Whadda *you* want?" the man snarled, swaying a little as he tried to focus his eyes on Shannon.

"Sorry friend. Fun's over. Let's take a walk."

The miner swore and grabbed clumsily at the handle of his six-gun. Shannon's Colt flashed through the air as he swung it at the miner's head. The gun barrel made a low-pitched, ugly sound as it struck the man's skull solidly just behind the left ear. The miner dropped to his knees and stayed there, holding his head in his hands and groaning. Just right, thought Shannon. Not hard enough to really hurt him, but hard enough to put him out of action. Maybe I haven't lost my touch after all. He jerked the old pistol out of the fallen man's holster and shoved it into his own belt, then straightened up and stared at Parker and Slade.

"Yeah, he's pretty tough all right, Parker," he said with undisguised sarcasm. "Your grandmother could have taken him."

"Uh, nice job, Sheriff," Parker mumbled sourly.

"Always glad to help out a taxpayer. Now, is there

anything else I can do for you, or is the show over for today?"

Parker sank his teeth further into his cigar and said nothing.

With one final glance around the room, Shannon reached down for the miner's collar, hauled him to his feet, and propelled him out through the swinging doors. Behind him a ripple of laughter erupted in the saloon, and as he passed through the doorway into the street he heard Parker snarling "Shut up, you stupid morons! I'll tell you when to laugh!"

When the miner was safely locked in one of the cells, Shannon tossed the keys to Pop Bentley and headed across the street. The restaurant had not yet opened for the evening meal, but when he knocked on the locked door Kathy Winters came to the front and let him in.

"I've brought you a little business if you want it," he said. "County's got a prisoner who has to be fed. Supper tonight and breakfast tomorrow, if he can eat with a lump on his head and a hangover. Can you do it?"

"Of course. I'll feed him so well he won't want to leave."

She came over just after sunset carrying a tray loaded with enough food for all of them. Pop Bentley took his own plate and the prisoner's into the jail, leaving Shannon and Kathy to eat at the desk. Shannon was surprised that she wanted to stay and eat with him.

"Not as nice as your place, I'm afraid," he said, looking around the dingy office. "I don't even have a tablecloth. And what about the restaurant? This is your busiest time of the day."

"It's the company that counts, not the tablecloth," she laughed. "And Mrs. Rodriguez is minding the restaurant for me this evening. What happened in the saloon today?"

"Parker tried to set me up. Got our friend back in the cell there all liquored up and then sent for me. I guess he wanted to see how I'd handle things. If he still thinks he can buy me he may have wanted to see a sample of what he was getting. Or maybe he was hoping I'd bungle it—kill the man, perhaps, and get the other miners down on me. Or maybe he was just plain hoping there'd be a fight, and I'd get plugged in the fracas, accidentally or otherwise. Most of the people in the room were his men, so it wouldn't have been hard to manage it."

Kathy Winters shook her head in dismay.

"You can't keep going up against those people alone, Mr. Shannon. There are too many of them, and they don't play by any rules."

"I've gone up against more and better men alone, Mrs. Winters. Of course," he added a little wistfully, "I was younger then."

"Have you been a lawman very long, Clay?"

"As long as I can remember, Mrs. Winters."

"Will you tell me about it sometime?"

"Sometime. There isn't much to tell."

But in fact there was a great deal to tell. As the sunset turned into twilight followed by starlight, they sat in chairs placed on the walk outside the office and talked in the darkness. Under Kathy Winters' gentle but persistent prodding he told her about himself, about things he had not thought would be of interest to anyone, even things he had half forgotten. He told her how it felt to be a deputy at the age of eighteen and a town marshal at twenty. He told her about his days in Dodge City, when he was a member of a city marshal's force that included some of the West's most famous names: Earp and the Masterson brothers, Charlie Bassett and the rest. He talked about the years he spent as a lawman in Abilene, Wichita, Caldwell, and other trail towns, trying to keep the lid on in places where Texas trailherds came flocking in each year and cowhands, gamblers, and gunmen met and mixed and fought in some of the toughest hell-holes on the frontier. And then, as he and Kathy Winters watched the rising moon climb over Whiskey Creek, Shannon told her about how it felt to be growing older year by year amid constant violence, while other men—good friends, good lawmen—fell in gunfights on dirty streets or in some pointless saloon encounter.

"And so," Kathy said gently, "you came south, trying to leave it all behind you."

"Yes," he said, "that's true. I was tired and I wanted . . . well, I wanted something more out of life than I'd found in any of those Kansas cowtowns."

He hesitated, uncertain as to whether he should continue. He had never spoken to anyone about these things before. Now, somehow, it seemed natural to talk about them to this young woman. He closed his eyes and leaned his chair back against the wall.

"One night in Caldwell," he said in a low voice, "a man I'd thrown in jail a couple of times waited for me in an alley with a shotgun. I put him down, but not before he'd fired a load of buckshot into my legs. It was six weeks before I could walk again."

Unconsciously, he touched his left knee, remembering.

"I had a lot of time to think then, flat on my back while the wounds healed, and I decided that I'd had enough of being a lawman, that somewhere, somehow, there must be something better. So I turned in my badge and rode out, looking for whatever it was I had missed in life."

"And then?"

"For about a year I drifted around, trying to find the answer. Trying to find myself, I suppose."

He bowed his head.

"I guess I was a fool," he said sadly.

Kathy Winters touched his hand.

"There's nothing wrong with wanting your life to have meaning," she said. "Everyone has doubts sometimes. Sooner or later, we all go searching for ourselves."

Shannon nodded in the darkness.

"Well, I guess I was no different from everyone else, then. But I made one big mistake—I just couldn't stop carrying the star. It's all I've ever known. Perhaps it's what I was born to do, I don't know. Anyway, when I rode into the county seat a few weeks back, I looked up Sheriff Hollister. We had worked together up north years ago. When he offered me a job, this job, I took it."

Shannon gave a rueful laugh.

"Hollister warned me it would be rough here, and I knew he was right. But I came anyway."

The woman was silent for a moment. When she spoke again, her voice was almost a whisper.

"Are you sorry you came?" she said softly.

Shannon looked over at her, suddenly conscious of the warmth of her body as she sat close beside him in the shadows.

"No," he said slowly, as much to himself as to her. "No, I'm not sorry at all. Now."

Chapter Six

The morning sun had barely risen above the hills when the miners arrived. Shannon was sitting at the desk doing some paperwork when their shadows filled the open doorway. He looked up and saw that there were four of them, and that the one in the lead was the big miner who had taken away the ambush victim's body on the day he had arrived in Whiskey Creek.

"Come in, gents," he said. "Sorry I don't have enough chairs for everybody." He got up and walked around to sit on the edge of the desk in front of them. "What can I do for you?"

"I'm John Talbert," said the big man. "We came down from the gold camp to have a word with you."

"Fine. What's on your mind?"

"You find out who killed old Joe yet?" Talbert said. There was an undercurrent of anger in his voice.

"No, not yet."

"You gonna find out?"

"If I can."

The miners exchanged glances.

Talbert said, "We hear you got Sam Spence locked up in your pokey."

"Big-built man with a beard? Yes, he's here."

"Why'd you arrest him?"

"Drunk and disorderly. What's this all about, Mr. Talbert?"

Talbert glanced at his friends and then fixed him with a piercing gaze.

"Look, Sheriff," he said, "us miners are just about fed up with this town. For one thing, our people keep getting jumped on the road down here. Half a dozen men from the gold camp have been robbed and killed on that trail in the past year—two in the past month. An' the law don't do nothing about it. Then when one of us gets a little drunk in town, he gets beat up by Ace Parker's hoodlums or thrown in jail with his head busted, like Sam. That's the way it's been for a long time. Seems like the law here is always on the side of people like Parker, and we get the short end."

He hesitated, then stared defiantly at the deputy.

"I guess what we want to know is, well, where do you stand? Just whose side are you on?"

Shannon took a deep breath.

"Let's get this straight right now, boys, once and for all," he said. "I'm not on anybody's side. I'm here to enforce the law to the best of my ability, and that means equally, for everybody. When I find out who's doing the killings, I'll go after the guilty parties, whoever they are."

One of the miners said "Aw, Sheriff, everybody knows it's Ace Parker and his bunch who've been doin' it."

"I don't *know* anything yet," snapped Shannon. "Neither do you. There's a difference between suspecting and knowing. When I know for sure, I'll move. Not before. As for your friend Spence, he was drunk, he tried to break up the saloon, he broke a bottle over another miner's head, and then he tried to draw on me. I could hold him for attempted murder, but I'm not going to. When he's finished sleeping it off this morning, he can walk out of here."

He stood up and faced them squarely, his arms folded.

"As far as the rest of you are concerned, this is how it is: I don't care if you come to town and raise a little dust on Saturday nights. As long as it's all in fun and nobody's in danger of getting seriously hurt, I'll stay out of it. I'm not going to make you check your guns when you come, either, because the way things are you need them for protection. But I don't want any unnecessary gunplay. The first man who draws a six-gun without just cause answers to me, whether he's a miner or a townsman or anybody else. All right?"

Talbert took a second before looking Shannon straight in the eye. "Okay, Sheriff," he said. "We didn't mean no offense."

"None taken," said Shannon. "Now, when you head back to the gold camp I'd appreciate it very much if you'd tell everyone up there what I've just said. Make sure everybody in the camp gets the word, so there won't be any misunderstandings next time they come to town. Will you do that for me?"

The miners mumbled agreement.

"Good," Shannon said. "Anything else, boys?"

They shuffled out of the office one by one. Talbert went last. As he reached the door he paused.

"Sheriff," he said, "if you need any help. . . ."

Shannon shook his head.

"Thanks, Mr. Talbert. I truly appreciate that. But this is my job, not yours. I just need a little time."

Talbert shrugged and followed the others out the door.

An hour later, Shannon told Pop Bentley to let Spence out of the cell. The miner came shuffling into the front office, a sheepish expression on his face.

"How's your head?" Shannon asked. The miner rubbed the back of his neck slowly.

"I've had worse. Thanks for knockin' some sense into me, Sheriff. Pop told me I made a fool of myself in the Lucky Lady last night. Sorry I tried to draw on you; that was a dumb thing to do. Another lawman mighta killed me for it."

"Don't worry about it," Shannon said. "I think you were being pushed into it. Let me guess—some of Parker's people were buying you a lot of drinks, right?"

"Yeah, that's right. Couple of the girls and two of his gunhands."

"They say anything about me?"

"Come to think of it, they did. Said you didn't like miners. Said you'd come after me if I got to havin' too much fun. Kept telling me I shouldn't take anythin' offa you. Jumpin' horned toads, they musta *wanted* me to take you on. An' I fell for it," he said angrily. "I must really have been drunk."

Shannon opened a drawer and handed him his worn gunbelt and the holster with the old percussion revolver in it.

"Not your fault," he said. "They were after me. Anyway, it's over now. Here, this is yours. Go on back to camp and forget about all of this."

"But Sheriff, they coulda gotten me *killed*."

"Go on back to camp, Sam. Leave Parker and his people to me."

The miner walked slowly out of the office, still mumbling to himself.

* * *

When the office clock chimed ten, Shannon picked up his hat and walked up the street. He passed the Lucky Lady without a glance and mounted the front steps of Mrs. Williamson's boardinghouse. As he was about to knock, the door opened and a man came stumbling out, clumsily stuffing his shirttail into his trousers. In his haste he almost collided with Shannon, who stepped back to give the man room.

"Blast it, mister," snarled the man, "look where you're. . . . Oh, sorry, Sheriff. Didn't see you." He looked up at the sky. "That sun's sure bright," he mumbled, pulling up his suspenders. "Like to have blinded me. Well, uh, gotta go. My wife's gonna wonder where I've been."

"She probably already knows," Shannon said mildly. The man gave him a frightened look and hurried off down the street.

"Well, well, well," declared a voice from the doorway. "Look who's here."

An impressive figure was standing in the open door, a massive woman clad in an equally large pink dressing gown. Her frizzy hair was an improbable red which clashed fiercely with the color of the gown.

"Mrs. Williamson?"

"As ever was. You're the new deputy, I suppose. Haven't seen one of your kind in these parts for a while."

"May I come in for a moment?"

The woman leered at him.

"Sure, honey. Always glad to see the law. Gives the place a little class."

Shannon stepped past her into a dimly lit hallway. To his right was a well-furnished parlor, to his left a stairway leading to the second floor.

"Most of the girls are asleep now," said Mrs. Williamson, looking Shannon over with unconcealed interest. "You have anybody particular in mind?"

"I'd like to speak to whoever has the second-floor room with the window that looks onto the alley."

Mrs. Williamson frowned.

"Angel?" she said guardedly. "What do you want with her?" Her eyebrows went up suddenly. "Don't tell me you want to take up where your friend Watkins left off."

"She and Watkins were friends?"

"Never mind that. Why do you want to see her?"

"I'd just like to speak with her."

The woman's expectant expression turned sour.

"They don't get paid to *talk*. Look, I ain't done nothing wrong. You got no call to come bargin' in here—"

"What's Angel's last name, Mrs. Williamson?"

"I ain't tellin' you *nothin'*, mister. You better get out of here."

Shannon regarded her coldly, then wheeled and started up the stairwell.

"Hey!" she cried, peering up the stairs after him. "You ain't got no right to. . . . This is Ace Parker's joint, mister, and you better not—"

Shannon paused at the top of the stairs and looked around him. The second-floor hall was even darker and seedier than the one below. An empty whiskey bottle lay on the floor near the top step, and he kicked it aside as he passed. Only one door could lead to the room with the window; he stopped before it and knocked.

"George!" bellowed Mrs. Williamson from the bottom of the stairwell. "Somebody get George! Quick!"

Shannon knocked again, louder.

"Come in," said a female voice. Shannon opened the door cautiously. The room was small and untidy, and it smelled of cheap perfume. A large brass bed dominated the available space; articles of clothing were draped over the furniture and spread over the floor. A bird-like young woman sat on the bed in her corset, running a hairbrush through her dark, disheveled hair. She was thin and pale, but she was still pretty under the makeup that was smeared across her face. Shannon saw that she was no more than eighteen or nineteen years old.

"May I come in?" he said. The girl said nothing, staring at him with frightened eyes. The sound of Mrs. Williamson's voice reached them from the stairwell.

"*George, get a move on!*" she screeched. Shannon closed the door of the room behind him.

"I'm sorry to bother you like this," he said to the girl. "I'm Clay Shannon. May I speak with you for a minute?"

Fear leaped into the girl's eyes as she saw the star on his shirt.

"I ain't done anything," she said.

"I know. I just want to talk to you. Your name is Angel?"

"Yes. Well, no. It's really Hilda. Hilda Gibbs. Angel's my, uh, professional name. Please, what've I done?"

"Nothing, Hilda. I need your help, that's all."

He moved to the window. A faded lace curtain hung across it; he moved it aside and looked out through the dusty glass. He was right above the area where Rodriguez had found Watkins' body. He let the curtain drop back again and turned back to face Hilda Gibbs.

"You were a friend of Mr. Watkins?" he asked gently.

She caught her breath. "Yes," she whispered, waiting.

Shannon sat down on the bed beside her and took her hands in his.

"Hilda," he said, smiling into her eyes, "were you up here in this room the night Mr. Watkins was killed?"

Her face went deathly pale.

"Yes . . . no . . . I mean . . . I don't remember." She pulled her hands away. "You mustn't ask me that," she said.

"Hilda, I'm trying to find the men who killed him. If you saw anything that night—"

"*No!*" She cried, turning away from him. "I don't want to talk about it. *Please* leave me alone!" She covered her face with her hands and began to cry.

The door crashed open. A hulking man stood slouched in the doorway, clad only in work boots and long red underwear. In his dangling right hand he was holding a scarred axe handle. His close-set eyes squinted myopically as he peered first at the sobbing girl, then at Shannon. The man reminded Shannon of an ape he had once seen in a traveling circus.

"What you doin' here, mister?" the man growled.

Shannon stood up and walked over to him, stopping only when he was toe to toe with the other man.

"You must be George," he said, staring levelly into the man's dull eyes.

"Well, yeah," said the man sullenly. His glance shifted momentarily around the room, then his jaw set and he scowled at Shannon.

"You got no business here. Mrs. W. wants you outta here, now."

"Go away, George," Shannon said softly. "I'm busy now. Tell Mrs. Williamson I'll be leaving soon."

Mrs. Williamson appeared behind George. There was fury on her face.

"You're leavin' *now*!" she screamed. "George, bash his fool head in!"

George put a hairy paw on Shannon's arm and raised the axe handle. Shannon shrugged, half-turned, then drove his left fist full force into George's midsection. George staggered backwards through the doorway, clutching his abdomen and gasping for breath. His buttocks crashed into the railing which guarded the stairwell; he fell over it and went tumbling down the stairs, yelping in pain, to land in a heap in the hallway below, clutching his stomach, moaning and cursing. The axe handle lay forgotten at Shannon's feet.

Mrs. Williamson glared at Shannon, darted a poisonous look at Hilda Gibbs, and fled down the hall toward the back of the house. Shannon turned back to the girl sitting on the bed.

"If Watkins was your friend," he said, "help me get whoever killed him. I know you saw something that night. Tell me. Quickly, before they come back."

"No, no, *no*!" she whimpered. "I can't. I just can't. They'd kill me."

"Who would kill you? *Quick, tell me*!"

She shook her head violently, her face contorted and wet with tears.

"Please go away, Sheriff," she whispered. "Leave me alone. Please, please, *please* leave me alone!"

Shannon sighed, then reached out and touched her shoulder.

"I understand," he said. "I'm sorry. I didn't realize how it was. Please forgive me."

He turned and went down the stairs, stepping over the still-prostrate George as he reached the lower floor and headed for the front entrance. Several women stood huddled in the hallway, watching him.

"*Ladies*," Shannon said, tipping his hat as he went out the door.

The bell over the restaurant door sounded cheerfully as Shannon entered the restaurant. It was just past noon, and several people were at the tables, eating. Kathy Winters came out of the kitchen wiping her hands on a dishtowel. Her smile was even warmer than Shannon remembered it.

"Have you got a minute?" he asked. She glanced at the people sitting at the tables, then drew Shannon back into the kitchen. Mrs. Rodriguez was stirring a large kettle which sat atop the wood-burning stove. She smiled briefly at Shannon, then returned to her work.

"What is it, Clay?" Kathy said, looking searchingly into his face. "I heard you had some trouble this morning with Mrs. Williamson's bouncer. Are you all right?"

"I'm fine. George is a little worse for the wear, though."

"You know you're making a lot of enemies . . ."

"And a few friends," he said. "Look, I'm sorry to bother you during the lunch hour, but I need to ask you something. Do you know anything about the relationship between Watkins and Hilda Gibbs?"

"Not much, I'm afraid. I didn't have much contact with either of them. There was talk, of course. Watkins spent a lot of time with Hilda at the Lucky Lady and at Mrs. Williamson's, but I'm not sure whether he was just buying her or whether it was more than that. Did she have something to do with his death?"

"I think she knows something about it. She may even have seen what happened. But she's afraid to talk about it."

"She may have good reason to be afraid. So may you."

"Things did get a little tense there for a bit." He grinned and rubbed his left hand. "It's a good thing George has slow reflexes."

Kathy shook her head impatiently.

"It's no joking matter, Clay," she said. "You can be sure Parker and Slade know by now you talked to that girl, and they won't like it."

"No," said Shannon, "they won't. But I'll have to

talk to her again anyway. She knows something—I'd bet on it. I'll wait a day or two to let things cool off, and then I'll try to find a way to speak with her somewhere besides the Lucky Lady or Mrs. Williamson's. Does she ever come in here?"

"No, never. The saloon girls keep pretty much to themselves."

"Well, thanks again for your help, Kathy," he said.

"No thanks necessary," she replied. "I'm glad to be a part of this. I guess I *need* to be a part of it."

He started to leave, but she touched his arm.

"Will you come back for supper? I'll save a steak for you. A big one."

Shannon looked at her with mock sternness. "Trying to bribe an officer of the law, ma'am?"

"I'll charge you double if it will make you feel better."

He laughed. It was the first time he had laughed out loud in a long time—a very long time. And it felt good.

"I'll be here," he said.

That afternoon Shannon went riding. He saddled up the buckskin and rode slowly through the streets of Whiskey Creek, noting the location of houses, stores, saloons, and all of the many other buildings which made up the town. He carefully filed away in his memory the layout of the side streets and alleys that ran between the many buildings, slowly forming a picture of what was where and how to get to it. He noted the location of front and back doors, and of doorways and windows where a man might lie in wait for another man. It was hard to remember it all, but he kept at it because, for a lawman in a strange town, there might come a time when such information could mean the difference between life and death.

Later he rode out into the hills above Whiskey Creek. Unhurriedly he examined the roads and trails leading into the town, then made his way slowly along the cliffs which overlooked it, taking in the details of the landscape. Now and then he paused to explore one of the myriad of rifts and gullies which cut through the rough hillsides. The buckskin stallion picked his way among the rocks without conscious urging from his rider, pricking his ears occasionally and blowing gently when the lawman patted his neck.

"Lot of country around here, partner," Shannon said, pausing at the top of the rimrock north of town. "Lots of places for somebody to hide who's up to mischief." The stallion tossed his head as if in agreement.

The sun was touching the horizon when they re-entered Whiskey Creek. Shannon's route back into town took him past the Lucky Lady, and although he was tired he straightened a little in the saddle and his eyes became watchful as he drew nearer to the saloon. For some reason, just being near the place made him uneasy.

His uneasiness swiftly proved justified. He was just a few yards away from the Lucky Lady when the swinging doors opened and Ace Parker came out. The saloonkeeper sauntered across the boardwalk and stood with his thumbs hooked in his vest, puffing on his cigar and watching Shannon's approach. As the stallion came abreast of the saloon, Parker stepped into the street and held up a hand.

"Hold it, Deputy," he said. "I wanna talk to you."

Shannon reined up beside him but did not dismount.

"Let's go inside," said Parker, waving his cigar at the Lucky Lady.

"Let's talk out here," said Shannon. "I'd feel safer."

Parker snorted, then looked around to see if anyone was within earshot. The street was deserted.

"Okay by me," Parker replied, shrugging his shoulders. He looked up at Shannon with an expression intended to be affable but which merely succeeded in being crafty.

"I been waiting for you to look me up," Parker said. "You did all right handling that drunk yesterday. I figured you had sand. That's the kind I want on my side—people with sand."

"Like Slade?"

"Slade's got plenty of sand, as you'll find out if you ever cross him," Parker growled. "Look, let's get down to cases. The other night I made you an offer. It still goes. It's worth five hundred a month to me for you to mind your own business around here. You don't have to gun anybody for me, or anything like that. You don't have to do a thing except look the other way at the right time. Five hundred a month, cash on the nail."

Shannon laughed and shook his head.

"Sorry, Parker," he said, "I don't come that cheap."

"Whaddaya mean, 'cheap'?" Parker rasped. "That's more money than you'll ever make wearin' that tin star." His jaw set angrily. "All right, how much does it take, then? What's your price?"

"More than you've got, Parker. I'm not for sale at any price. Neither is this badge."

Parker tossed his cigar away and pointed a finger at Shannon. He was trembling with fury.

"Now you listen to me," he snarled. "This is my town and in my town there are only two kinds of people—those that are with me and those that are against me. That applies to you too. If you ain't my friend, you're my enemy. There's no middle road. Now what about it—are you in or out?"

Shannon straightened up in the saddle and picked up the reins.

"Parker, as far as I'm concerned, you get treated like any other citizen. No blind eye, no favors. Obey the law and I'll protect you from those who don't. Break the law and you'll answer for it. If that means

I'm out, then I'm out." He nudged the buckskin into a walk, forcing Parker to step hastily out of the way.

"You just made a big mistake, mister!" Parker yelled. "A *big* mistake!" He cursed and rushed angrily back into the Lucky Lady.

Shannon put the tired buckskin into the stable behind the jail. Despite his own weariness, he took the time to rub the horse down and feed it, then turned it out into the little corral and walked up the alley to the office. Pop Bentley was just getting ready to lock up.

"Everything quiet today, Pop?" Shannon said. The old man nodded.

"Peaceful as a Sunday school picnic," he said. "Think I'll go feed my hogs for excitement." He limped off toward his shack.

Shannon locked the office door behind him and crossed the street. He wanted a steak and Kathy Winters' company—not necessarily in that order.

It was dark when he came out of the restaurant. He paused on the walk for a moment, enjoying the memory of the meal. The restaurant had been so busy that Kathy had not been able to sit with him, but he had taken pleasure in a leisurely supper and the opportunity to unwind after the long day.

He thought of his encounter in the street with Parker. He was not unduly troubled by the incident with the saloonkeeper because he had been expecting it, but it was apparent that henceforth he would have to be doubly alert. Parker was an arrogant loudmouth, but now that he was certain the deputy could not be bought off he would be dangerous. Not personally, perhaps—Parker was not the kind to do his own killing. But he had Slade and a half-dozen other gunmen, and Shannon was alone. When would they make their move? And how?

The answer came quickly. The bellow of the six-gun was like a physical blow, jarring him from his reverie and sending his heart racing wildly. There were two shots, and they came from behind the jail—Shannon saw the reflection of the muzzle flashes on the walls of the nearby buildings. Colt in hand, he charged across the street and crouched at the rear corner of the jail, searching the darkness for the source of the firing.

A man broke from behind the stable and darted up the alley which ran up the hill toward the Lucky Lady. As he crossed the open space he fired twice at Shannon—the slugs ripped splinters off the jail wall, stinging the deputy's cheek. Shannon got off one quick shot as the racing figure passed through a patch of light; the man stumbled, then regained his balance and continued on up the dark alley. By the time Shannon rounded the corner there was no one in sight.

He started back past the stable, reloading the Colt. What had the man been shooting at? Not at him, not at first. The initial shots had not been fired in his direction. Then what . . . ?

He stopped and stared at the corral. The buckskin stallion lay motionless on his side in the dust. With a curse Shannon leaped over the corral fence and knelt down beside the fallen animal. Unmindful of the danger, he lit a match and held it up.

The stallion was dead. Two bloody holes gaped in his right side, just behind the shoulder. Shannon stared at them until the match burned his fingers. He lit another.

Slowly he ran his hand along the buckskin's sleek neck. It was still soft, still warm, but there was no responsive toss of the big head, no familiar whinny of affection to greet him, nor would there ever be again. He got to his feet and gazed down at the dead animal; they'd been together a long time, had ridden many trails together.

Suddenly, Shannon felt very old and very tired. He had few friends in the world, and one of them lay dead at his feet. Now he was more alone than ever.

Someone came around the corner of the stable toward him. He brought the muzzle of the Colt up, then relaxed as he recognized Pedro Rodriguez.

Rodriguez looked at the dead horse and then at the lawman.

"I heard the shots and saw the man run away up the alley," he said. "Are you hurt?"

"No," Shannon said. "He missed me."

"In that case," said Rodriguez, "you must have wounded the man when you fired at him. There is blood by the corner of the building, just there." He pointed toward the rear of the building across the alley from the stable.

Shannon climbed back over the corral fence and strode to the place Rodriguez had indicated. There a patch of light from a nearby window fell across the alley, and in the center of the illuminated area Shannon saw red stains spattered across the ground. The blood trail led away up the alley—and toward the rear of the Lucky Lady Saloon.

Bitterness welled up in Shannon. The Lucky Lady again, always the Lucky Lady. Parker had struck quickly, and in a manner worthy of the man: by sending some hireling to sneak down an alley and shoot a horse under cover of darkness.

"Thanks, Mr. Rodriguez," he said. "I'll take a look."

He slipped into the shadows behind the buildings and began to move cautiously along the alley. A honky-tonk piano's notes drifted down from the Lucky Lady, helping to cover the sound of his footsteps. Had the gunman made it to the saloon and safety? Or was he hiding somewhere in the darkness, waiting?

The question was answered abruptly as the flash and roar of a six-gun filled the alley a few yards ahead. The bullet tugged at Shannon's shirt as it went by.

The man had risen up from behind some discarded crates and was cocking his revolver for a second shot when Shannon fired. The man screamed and fell. Shannon vaulted over the crates and leveled his Colt to shoot again, then saw that the man was writhing on the ground, his gun lying beside him. Shannon kicked the weapon away and bent over the wounded man, grabbing him roughly by the shirt and jerking him into a sitting position. The man was gasping for breath and moaning, and Shannon could see that the bullet had hit him in the stomach.

"Who are you, mister?" Shannon snarled, shaking him by the shirtfront. The man groaned.

"Get me to the doc," he gasped. "My belly's on fire."

Several people had come out of their back doors to see what was happening, and Shannon yelled at one of them to go get the doctor. Pedro Rodriguez came up with a lighted lamp. Shannon took it and held it over the wounded gunman.

"Any of you know this man?" Shannon said to the crowd gathering around.

"Don't know his name," said someone, "but I think he works for Ace Parker."

"Yeah," said someone else, "I seen him up at the Lucky Lady before."

"His name is Ziebart," Rodriguez said. "He is Parker's man."

Shannon put his face close to the wounded man's.

"Did Parker send you down here?" he barked. "Answer me! *Did Parker send you?*"

Ziebart looked at him with pain-filled eyes.

"Get away," he said, and died.

Shannon watched without emotion as the town's alcoholic doctor examined the corpse.

"Deader than a doornail," said the doctor at length, closing his black bag. "One in the leg, one in the gut. Nice shooting, Deputy."

Shannon handed the lamp back to Pedro Rodriguez and began to search the body. The pants pockets yielded only a jackknife, some coins, and a plug of tobacco, but in the pocket of the shirt he found a small leather bag secured by a drawstring. The bag was flat and seemed to be empty, but he opened it anyway. Something gleamed in the lamplight, and he realized that the inside of the bag was coated with specks of gold. He inspected the outside of the bag more closely, and saw that the letters "J. G." had been burned into the leather. He pocketed the bag and walked back to the corral, leaving the doctor to dispose of the body.

Several people had gathered in the stable area. Shannon sent them about their business. He was standing alone at the corral fence, thinking, when Pop Bentley came up. Bentley leaned on the top rail of the corral and shook his head.

"Takes a poor excuse of a man to shoot down a horse out of sheer meanness," Pop said.

"It wasn't just meanness, Pop, it was a message. From Parker to me."

"Yeah," said the older man, "that's Parker's style, right enough. You had that animal long?"

"Ten years, nearly eleven. We covered a lot of miles together, and he never let me down once."

He looked up at the stars. Had there been more light, a close observer might have noticed the pain in his eyes, but it was dark and there was no one to see or share his grief.

"Pop," he said at length, "there's something I've got to do first thing in the morning. It won't wait. I wish it could, but it can't. Do you think you could take care of the buckskin for me?"

"Sure, son," Bentley replied. "I'll take him out beyond the edge of town in the mornin' and bury him under the cottonwoods. Some nice spots down there— shady and peaceful-like. I'll get a coupla boys to help me."

Pedro Rodriguez came out of the alley.

"I'll give you a hand, Pop," he said.

Chapter Seven

When Shannon awoke the next morning he went into the jail and looked out the back window at the corral. It was empty, Bentley and Rodriguez had come early for the buckskin. He shaved and dressed, picked up his saddle and rifle, and headed down the hill to the livery stable to hire a horse.

"Yeah," said the owner of the stable, "I heard about your stallion. Real shame—that was a fine-lookin' animal. I got a little sorrel here that might do you. She ain't as big as your horse was, but she's sound and smart."

"I may need her for quite awhile," Shannon said.

"She's yours as long as you want her."

He saddled the mare and rode out of town toward the gold camp. The road was wide but deeply rutted; many wagons had passed up and down it carrying supplies to the miners in the hills.

As he climbed up the winding trail Shannon twice passed riders headed down toward town. The second

man was Spence, the miner he had released from jail
just the day before.

"Morning, Sam," Shannon said as they passed.
"Headed for town?"

"Yeah," said Spence, not meeting his eyes.

"Stay out of trouble, Sam. And stay out of the
Lucky Lady."

"Okay, Sheriff," Spence said, riding on.

The road followed the gorge through which ran the
small river from which the town below had derived its
name. Down in the valley, where it wound among the
cottonwood trees, the stream was broader and moved
more slowly, and there it was known as Whiskey
Creek; but here in the hills it was called the Swiftwater
River, and it had earned its name. Fed by the snows
of the far mountains, it raced and plunged down its
steep bed toward the valley below. The cold, clear
water gurgled invitingly as it rushed past, and twice
Shannon stopped to drink deeply.

But even as he drank, he kept a constant watch on
the slopes above him, knowing that any rider on this
road would be an easy target for a marksman hidden
in the rocks. The journey was a long one, and every
mile brought him within rifle range of a thousand
places where a man might lie in wait. At every turn
the way was overhung by steep cliffs, barren and rock-
strewn, which rose menacingly above the road to rims
broken by endless clefts and crevices where an army

might easily have been hidden. Along the road itself there was little cover for anyone under attack from the rimrock; Shannon was not surprised that more than one man had been found dead along that barren trail. It was with some relief when, just before noon, he rounded the last bend and started down into the gold fields.

The mining camp was a little community of tents and crude shacks lining the last few hundred feet of road and spreading out alongside the slopes beyond. There were no miners in sight—they would all be at work further upstream—but a few bedraggled women looked out of tent flaps or peered through shack windows as he rode by. Ahead of him he saw a tent larger than the rest. The words WIMMIN AND LICKER HEAR were splashed across its canvas wall in black paint. A gray-haired woman, hugely fat and clothed only in a stained shift, was standing in front of the tent. She was puffing contentedly on a long black cigar as Shannon rode up. He asked for directions to the claim of John Talbert, politely refused the lady's offer of entertainment at a reasonable price, and then climbed up a narrow, muddy track to the spot she had indicated.

Talbert was there, repairing a flume. He put down his hammer and waited silently for his visitor to dismount.

"Mornin'," he said finally. "Didn't expect you to be

comin' up this way." His tone was neither friendly nor hostile.

"I passed Sam Spence on the trail," Shannon said, tying up the mare.

"Yeah," said Talbert. "He was hoppin' mad at Parker's bunch for getting him into trouble the other day. He headed for town early this morning. Hope he don't do nothin' foolish. That what you came up here to talk about?"

Shannon reached into his pocket and pulled out the little leather bag he had taken from Ziebart's body.

"*This* is what I came up here to talk about," he said, "Do you recognize it?" Talbert took the bag and looked at it closely, turning it over twice before opening it to look inside. He pulled the drawstring shut again and handed back the bag.

"That's the little poke old Joe Grubbs used to carry. Those are his initials on the side of it. I saw him burn the letters in myself. Where'd you find it?"

"In a dead man's pocket."

"It's nigh on noon," said Talbert, looking at the sun. "Come on up to the tent and let's have a bite to eat. I'd like to hear about this."

Over a spartan lunch Shannon told Talbert what had happened. The miner listened with growing anger.

"This could hang Parker," he said finally.

"No," said Shannon. "It could have hung Ziebart, but he's past hanging now. If I'd caught him alive, he might have told me enough so that I could arrest Parker, but when he cut loose at me in the alley I didn't have time to talk. Without him there's no way to prove that Parker ordered Grubbs killed. Ziebart could have gone after Grubbs on his own. For that matter, he could have found the bag somewhere or won it in a poker game or come into possession of it in some other way. That's what a lawyer would argue in court, anyway. Unless one of the others talks, chances are a judge would turn Parker loose for lack of evidence."

Talbert's face darkened with anger.

"How much evidence do you need before you can kill a snake?" he said. "Just blow his head off and be done with it. Nobody around here would fault you. You're the law, ain't you?"

"No, Mr. Talbert," Shannon said, "I'm *not* the law. I'm just one of the people who are sworn to uphold it. And the law I'm sworn to uphold says that before I can take Parker down, I've got to have more proof."

"Then it looks like you've had a long ride for nothin'."

"Maybe," said Shannon. He rose and extended his hand. "Thanks for your time."

"What are you going to do now, Sheriff?"

Shannon shrugged.

"I don't know," he said. "Yet."

* * *

The trip back through the hills was easier than the ascent. Again he stopped along the way to drink from the rushing stream and to water the mare.

A mile above Whiskey Creek the road wound through huge bluffs that towered menacingly over the track. Shannon was riding through the sharpest part of the turn when he heard the flat crack of a rifle above and behind him, and a bullet kicked up dust beneath the sorrel's feet. Cursing himself for his lack of vigilance, Shannon kicked free of the stirrups and rolled out of the saddle just as another bullet sang past. He hit the ground hard, so hard that the impact drove the breath momentarily from his body. Gasping, he leaped up and dived into a cleft between some boulders just beside the road, the only cover within reach. The sorrel mare, startled by the shot and his sudden exit from the saddle, danced away down the trail a few feet and then stood with reins dragging, tossing her head nervously.

In the shelter of the rocks Shannon drew his Colt and searched the hillside for some sign of his attackers. After several seconds he detected a slight movement on the rim almost directly above him. He aimed carefully and fired, and was rewarded by a shrill yell of pain. Immediately a second rifle opened up on him from another point a few yards further along the crest. Bullets snapped past his face, ricocheting off the sides of the cleft and whining away into space. Two rifles against a six-gun—bad odds at that distance.

He looked longingly at the Winchester in the scabbard on the mare's saddle and called to her, trying to coax her over. She pawed the ground but did not come to him, and he thought fleetingly of the dead buckskin—the stallion had been trained to come when called.

But the sorrel remained beyond reach, and so did the rifle, and there was nothing he could do about it. With two rifles covering him, if he tried to make a dash for the mare he would almost surely be cut down before he had covered half the distance. He would have to make the six-gun do.

He raised his head again, hoping to get a glimpse of the second gunman, but the result was three quick shots which slapped into the rocks near his head and then buzzed angrily away after bouncing off the walls of the cleft. He realized with growing desperation that while he could not safely leave the cover of the rocks, neither could he stay where he was. The cleft was too shallow, and he was too exposed. Eventually a ricochet would get him even if he kept down. And to make things worse, as he surveyed the cliff face he saw that there was a large crevice in the cliff wall directly in front of him that led straight up to the rim. If the drygulchers worked their way along the top of the cliff to the head of that little defile they would have a clear shot at him. Right or wrong, he must do something, and quickly.

Bracing himself, he loosed two shots at the rimrock where the second rifle was stationed, then scrambled hurriedly out of the cleft and began climbing up the crevice in the cliff. It was steep and treacherous, and he clawed for handholds as his boots slipped and scrabbled on the smooth rock. His breathing became labored and his muscles ached with the effort, but he dared not stop to rest. If the bushwhackers reached the head of the crevice before he did, there would be no escape for him; trapped, he would die quickly under their guns.

More shots echoed to his left, and faintly behind him he heard the splat of bullets in the hiding place he had just left. Luck was with him—they had not seen him leave the cleft in the boulders below. They thought he was still down there, by the road. He had a chance.

He was within ten feet of the top, sobbing for breath and nearly exhausted, when a man armed with a rifle appeared suddenly on the rim above him. A bloody bandanna was tied around the man's left arm, a testament to Shannon's earlier marksmanship. As he came into view the rifleman was looking back toward someone else who was out of sight over the rim.

"You keep him covered from there," the man shouted over his shoulder. "I'll get behind him." He turned, then let out a yell of surprise as he found Shannon confronting him only a few feet away. Clearly he had not expected to meet his intended victim at such close quarters. He raised the rifle to shoot, but Shannon was quicker. The Colt jumped in his hand. The heavy .45 slug was aimed at the man's chest but struck the trigger housing of the rifle instead, mangling two of the bushwhacker's fingers and splintering the rifle's stock. The man screamed, dropped the rifle, and bolted out of sight.

Cursing, Shannon drove himself up the last few feet to the top, crawled over the edge, and scrambled to his feet. To his astonishment he saw that the wounded attacker, rather than waiting to cut him down at short range, was now some distance away and in full flight toward two horses tethered in the brush. As Shannon appeared, the second rifleman jumped up from among the rocks, his mouth gaping open in astonishment. He fired a wild shot in the deputy's direction and then dashed headlong after his companion. Shannon managed to get off one shot at long range, but he was still gasping for breath and his hand was unsteady after the physical exertion of the climb. Before he could even cock the Colt's hammer for a second shot the two gunmen had flung themselves into their saddles and set off at a furious gallop. Within seconds they had vanished into a distant arroyo.

Shannon sank to his knees and reloaded the six-gun. When his breathing had returned to nearly normal, he climbed to his feet again and walked to the head of the arroyo. He had half-hoped the ambushers might have stopped there to put up a fight, but they had gone, and it would be pointless to pursue them. Afoot, it would be impossible for him to catch up to them, even assuming he could pick up their trail on the rocky ground. Reluctantly he turned and walked back along the bluff.

Several cartridge cases littered the ground around the spot where the gunmen had opened fire on him. He examined them briefly, noting that they were of the same caliber as the ones he had found near the old miner's body on the trail coming into Whiskey Creek. They could have been from the same rifle, or they could have been from a different weapon—there was no way for him to tell. He had heard that experts in the East could now sometimes match a cartridge case to the gun that had fired it, but he had no such expertise available to him. He pocketed the spent casings anyway.

The rest of his search yielded nothing, which meant there was nothing to connect the two men with Parker. He had not recognized them. Could they have been drifters, looking for a quick and easy mark along the road from the gold camp? Or had they been sent by Parker to kill him?

He climbed stiffly back down to the road, trying to suppress his disgust. After all that's happened, he thought, I still have no proof of anything. But at least I'm still alive. For now.

He walked to the place in the road where the sorrel mare stood waiting for him. Dragging himself into the saddle, he took up the reins and started slowly toward Whiskey Creek.

Dusk was falling when he reached town. In the homes and businesses oil lamps were already being lit, and squares of light from the windows made bright patterns in the street as he rode by. He saw that the office was dark—Pop Bentley had apparently gone back home to his hogs—so he rode on down to the livery stable, put away the mare, and then walked back up to the office. He paused at the door, looking over at the restaurant. Through the window he could see that the dining room was full, every table occupied. Mrs. Rodriguez was visible moving from table to table, but there was no sign of Kathy Winters. No doubt she was busy in the kitchen. He decided to go over later when the place was not so crowded.

He had just opened the office door when pandemonium erupted. Someone was shouting in the Lucky Lady; there was the sound of furniture breaking, and a woman screamed. Shannon slipped the thong off the hammer of his six-gun, slammed the office door behind him, and started up the street. Before he had taken a dozen steps there was more yelling from the saloon and a shot rang out, then another. A man came staggering through the swinging doors of the saloon; he stumbled off the boardwalk into the street, doubled over and clutching at his belly. Another man came through the door with a six-gun in his hand. Shannon saw what was about to happen and shouted a warning, but it was too late—the second man raised his revolver, aimed carefully at the wounded man's back, and fired twice. The victim jerked violently as the heavy slugs hit him, then collapsed face down in a patch of lamplight and lay still.

Shannon strode up to the shooter and wrenched the six-gun out of his hand, covering him with his own Colt as he did so. He saw that it was one of Parker's hirelings, a scrawny little man who claimed his name was Smith. The gunman yelped with pain as the revolver was twisted out of his grasp.

"Stay put, Smith," Shannon said. "Move a muscle and I'll drop you." Keeping Smith covered, he backed off the walk and knelt down beside the fallen man. Rolling him over, he saw that it was Sam Spence. The miner was dead.

As he rose to his feet, people were coming out of the Lucky Lady and spreading out along the sidewalk. Seeing the deputy's drawn gun, they kept well clear of Smith, who stood silently rubbing his sore fingers.

"You're under arrest, Smith," Shannon said. "Walk down here with your hands in plain sight."

"Wait a minute, Deputy," said a hoarse voice from the saloon doorway. It was Parker.

"Come on, Smith," said Shannon. I won't tell you again." Smith moved into the street and stood glaring at him malevolently.

"I said *hold it*," Parker roared. "What are you arresting my man for?"

"For murder, Parker," Shannon said, removing a hide-out gun from Smith's right boot. "Even you ought to be able to figure that one out."

"But it was a fair fight!" Parker cried. "Spence drew first! He came in here all likkered up again and started yellin' about us tryin' to get him killed. Smitty tried to quiet him down, but Spence drew on him, and Smitty had to shoot in self-defense. Ain't that the way it was, boys?" There was a rumble of agreement from the crowd.

A lump was forming in Shannon's stomach. He was standing squarely in the light streaming out of the saloon doorway, but all he could see of the people on the walk were their silhouettes. He was an easy target if anybody in the crowd wanted to kill him. Moving deliberately, he took Smith by the arm and maneuvered the gunman between himself and the crowd on the walk.

"What happened in the saloon may have been self-defense," he said, "but what I saw in the street wasn't." He shoved Smith in the direction of the jail, still keeping him in the line of fire. Three or four men came off the walk into the street, following them, their hands close to their guns.

"Back off, you men!" Shannon barked. They hesitated, then came on. Several of them broke into a run down the boardwalk, trying to outflank him. He felt a film of perspiration forming on his forehead. They were going to cut him off from the jail, and there were too many of them.

"Give it up, Deputy!" Parker yelled. "You'll never make it!" Shannon pushed Smith onward. Some of the pursuers were now between him and the jail. If just one of them drew a gun, he would have to fight with the odds badly against him.

At that very moment two of the men started to reach for their six-guns. Shannon cocked his Colt and braced himself.

The sudden blast of the shotgun was like a blow in the stomach. The muzzle flash lit up the entire street, and the noise was deafening. Shannon whirled in the direction of the explosion as Parker's men froze in their tracks. The sound of two new shells being dropped into the shotgun's chambers and the click of the gun being snapped shut again echoed clearly along the street.

"Who the devil is that?" said someone.

Pedro Rodriguez stepped out of the shadows into a patch of light. The double-barreled twelve-gauge shotgun in his hands had been pointed skyward; now it swept smoothly down to cover the men blocking Shannon's path.

"All right, *amigos*," Rodriguez said. "Move back onto the sidewalk—slowly. That's right. You two—just let those *pistolas* slip back into their holsters and keep your hands where I can see them." The men did as they were told. "Ah, that's much better. Thank you. Now, whenever you're ready, Sheriff."

Shannon propelled his reluctant prisoner past Rodriguez up onto the walk and kicked open the door to his office, thankful that the lamp was not lit to backlight him. Keeping Smith between himself and the crowd, he waited while Rodriguez backed slowly onto the walk and stood beside him, still holding the shotgun on the men in the street. Shannon heard footsteps coming up the walk behind him and turned to cover the threat, only to see Pop Bentley come limping out of the darkness.

"Heard the shootin'," Bentley said. "Since you come to town, shootin' means there's work to be done. Figured you might need me."

"Evening, Pop," said Shannon. "Would you be kind enough to show Mr. Smith to his accommodations?"

Bentley chuckled and hustled Smith ahead of him into the jail. Shannon turned and stepped back onto the walk to look closely at the men facing him. He wanted to make certain that he would remember their faces later.

"All right, you people," he said loudly. "Fun's over. Anyone on this street three minutes from now gets to share a cell with Smith. Now move out, all of you, nice and easy." He waited, hardly daring to breathe, while the men hesitated, making up their minds whether to draw or walk away.

Then Parker's voice came down the street from the door of the Lucky Lady.

"Okay, boys," he snarled, "come on back. He's won this round." He shook his fist. "This ain't over yet, Deputy," he bellowed.

Grumbling and moving slowly, the crowd drifted back toward the saloon. "Don't worry, Smitty," someone called, "we'll get you out."

"I said *move*," Shannon snapped.

When the street was clear, he lowered his Colt and took a deep breath. Rodriguez carefully eased down the hammers on the shotgun, then took off his hat and wiped a handkerchief around the inside of the sweatband.

"A little warm for this time of year, no?" he said.

"You took a big chance, my friend," Shannon said. "That could have gotten ugly, and it wasn't even your fight. Thanks."

Rodriguez showed his teeth.

"It was my pleasure, *amigo*. You fight for all of us.

The least I can do is be of some small assistance. Besides, it was nothing. I just happened along."

"Sure, you just happened along—with a loaded shotgun. Come on in."

When the door and shutters had been closed, Shannon lit the lamp and turned it down low.

"You know," he said to Rodriguez, "for a peace-loving average citizen you were pretty cool out there just now. I think you've been in that kind of a spot before. You ever carry the star?"

Rodriguez propped the shotgun against the door-frame and sighed.

"It was a long time ago," he said. "But once, yes, like you I was a lawman. It was in San Antonio, when I was young. I had almost forgotten what it feels like to back down a gang of *puercos* like that."

Pop Bentley came through the jail door into the office.

"Hey," he said, "it's an insult to my livestock to call that bunch pigs. Rats, maybe, or lice. They ain't good enough to be pigs."

Someone knocked urgently at the door. Shannon slid his gun out of its holster and motioned the others to move back.

"Who is it?" he said loudly.

"Kathy Winters, Clay. Let me in." Shannon blew out the lamp and opened the door. When Kathy was safely inside he closed the door again and relit the lamp.

"I saw it all, Clay," she said in a strained voice. "It was terrifying. Are you all right—all of you?"

"We're fine, Kathy," he said, "thanks to Mr. Rodriguez. Look, you'd better not stay here. I don't think there'll be any more trouble tonight, but we can't count on that. Go on back, and I'll see you in the morning."

He turned to Rodriguez.

"You too, *amigo*—go home. Pop and I will mind the store. If anyone bothers you or your family tonight, fire a shot. I'll hear it and come running." He handed Rodriguez his shotgun. "Now go on, both of you. Pete, thanks again. You saved my neck tonight. I owe you."

He blew out the lamp once more and let Rodriguez and Kathy out. When he saw that Kathy was safely across the street he closed and bolted the door. Pop Bentley went into the jail carrying a blanket for his bunk, closing the heavy door behind him.

Shannon took one of the office shotguns out of the rack behind the desk, loaded it, and sat down on the bunk. Placing the shotgun over his knees he pulled the pillow up against the wall, leaned back, and prepared himself for a wakeful night.

Chapter Eight

He awoke with a start. Pop Bentley was opening the shutters on the office windows. The daylight streamed in.

"What time is it?" Shannon mumbled.

"Bit after six," said Bentley. "You sit up all night?"

He acknowledged that he had. It must have been three or four when he had drifted off to sleep. He had expected Parker to make some move to rescue his man from the jail, but nothing had happened. He stretched his cramped muscles, then carried the shotgun over to the wall rack.

"You want some breakfast?" Pop said. "I got a coupla cans of beans and a campstove back there in the jail."

Shannon declined the offer. His back hurt and there was a foul taste in his mouth, and he was in no mood for beans. He accepted a cup of steaming coffee and, after two quick swallows, opened the front door carefully and looked out. A few yards up the street two of

105

Parker's men were lounging on the walk, keeping an eye on the office. In a doorway across the street was another. Shannon handed Bentley the coffee cup, then stepped out onto the walk and strode over to the two men standing on his side of the street.

"Get going," he said.

"Why? We ain't breakin' no law," said one sulkily. Shannon drew his Colt, cocked it, and placed the muzzle against the man's fat stomach.

"You're breaking *my* law," he growled. "Now you and this other little weasel here just scoot on back up to the saloon and tell your boss I don't like his mangy *pistoleros* hanging around watching me. And take your friend across the street there with you."

"You wouldn't shoot me just for standin' here," the man protested.

"You're wrong," Shannon growled. "I gut-shot one of your sneaking yellow friends the other night, and I enjoyed it. I'd like to try it again on somebody, and you'll do just fine." Out of the corner of his eye he saw the man across the street sliding his hand toward his holster.

"Mister," he continued, pressing the muzzle of the gun harder against the man's stomach, "if you want to live longer than the next five seconds, you'd better tell that coyote across the street there to take his hand off of that gun and get on up the street. *Do it.*"

"Hey, Bill," the fat man called shrilly. "Hold it. We

don't want no trouble. We're goin' back to the saloon."

"When you get there, stay there," Shannon said. "The next one of your gang I see staking out my office is going either to jail or to Boot Hill, and I don't much care which. Now start moving."

The three men scurried up the street and vanished into the Lucky Lady.

When Shannon got back to the office Pop Bentley was standing on the walk waiting for him.

"Jumpin' jackrabbits," Bentley said, shaking his head in wonder. "Would you really have shot that *hombre* just for being there?"

Shannon thought of his dead horse.

"Yes," he said. "I would."

At eleven o'clock that morning Sam Spence was buried on Boot Hill.

Whiskey Creek's sizeable burial ground covered the top of a hillock just east of town. The tall gateway of the cemetery stood at the crest of the hill, silhouetted against the sky like a gallows. The graves had been dug without system or order, so that the wooden crosses erected above them seemed to be scattered randomly over the ground. Some of the crosses had names carved or burned into them, but many were unmarked and more than one bore only the epitaph, UNKNOWN. Whiskey Creek was that kind of a town.

A dozen of Spence's friends gathered at the cemetery shortly before eleven. Fearing trouble, Shannon reluctantly saddled the sorrel mare and rode out to the hill to keep an eye on the proceedings. He left Pop Bentley locked in the office with strict instructions to watch Smith like a hawk and to open the door of the jail for no one.

It had begun to rain at mid-morning, and as Shannon walked the mare up the little road to the cemetery gate her hoofs squelched noisily in the deepening mud. The rain and grey sky were a fitting backdrop for the occasion.

He found the assembled miners huddled together just inside the gate, their clothes wet and bedraggled, dripping water into the puddles around their feet.

Someone had knocked together a crude coffin out of used boards, and Spence, securely nailed inside, was escorted to his last resting place on the back of a buckboard. The miners removed their hats as the wagon trundled into the cemetery and stopped beside the waiting grave.

Shannon sat astride the sorrel a short distance away and watched as the coffin was lowered clumsily into the hole. There was no preacher in Whiskey Creek, and none of the miners could think of anything to say. After an awkward moment of silence, they wordlessly began to shovel the wet dirt over the coffin.

Three riders came up the road from town, plodding

purposefully through the mud. When they were still a hundred yards away Shannon recognized them as Parker's men. They guided their horses through the cemetery gate and reined up a few yards from the miners, who watched their approach with ill-concealed animosity.

The riders eased themselves in their saddles and grinned broadly at the little group of mourners.

"Phew," said one of the horsemen loudly to his companions, "it really stinks up here. Somethin' musta died."

"Nah." said one of the others, "these mud-miners always smell like that. Almost as bad as sheep."

"Worse," said the third rider. "Especially the one they're plantin'."

One of the miners who had been shoveling dirt into the hole stopped his work and walked over to the horsemen.

"Get out of here, you scum," he snarled, "or we'll put you in the hole with him."

Shannon quickly moved the sorrel forward and interposed himself between the miner and the three riders.

"That's enough of that," he snapped. He looked at the Parker hands. "You men have no business here," he said. "Ride out, now." He turned to the miner with the shovel. "You—go back over there and let's get on with the burying."

"Yeah, get on with it," yelled one of the riders. "The sooner you cover him up the sooner he'll stop stinkin' up the place."

The miner ducked under the neck of the sorrel, ran up to the rider who had just spoken, and swung the shovel with all of his strength into the man's face. The horse reared in fright and the rider went over backwards out of the saddle; he lay writhing on the wet ground, moaning and clutching at his head. The other miners whooped and started forward. The two Parker men who were still in their saddles went for their guns. Shannon knocked the shovel-wielding miner to the ground with the barrel of his .45 and spurred the mare forward into the two riders' horses. The animals reared and bucked. One of the men lost his seat and fell with a splash into the mud. Instantly the deputy covered the other one with the Colt.

"I said *that's enough*," he shouted. "Put the gun away. You on the ground—help your friend back into the saddle. Move!"

Cursing and muttering, the dismounted Parker men climbed back into their saddles. The man who had been hit with the shovel sat unsteadily on his horse, wiping the blood from his face with his neckerchief. He had a cut on his forehead, and his broken nose was bleeding profusely.

"That crazy miner like to have killed me, Sheriff," he mumbled through swollen lips.

"You came up here to make trouble, and you got it," Shannon said angrily, "so don't start crying to me about it. Now quit whining and get on out of here."

Grumbling, the riders began to turn their horses.

The other miners were helping up the man Shannon had knocked down.

"All right," Shannon said to the miner, "I didn't hit you that hard. Pick up the shovel. The rest of you, let's get back over there and finish the funeral." He crowded the miners with his horse, chivvying them away from the riders. Slowly they backed up, still glowering at the horsemen.

"We'll remember this," one of the Parker men yelled as he wheeled his horse to ride away.

"Good," Shannon snapped. "Then we won't have to do it all over again."

The three riders started back down the hill, casting sullen glances over their shoulders. Shannon watched to make sure none of them decided to draw a weapon as they retreated.

Suddenly the flat boom of a shotgun came echoing up out of Whiskey Creek.

"Now what?" growled one of the miners.

Shannon swore and wheeled the mare toward the cemetery gate. He put her into a gallop, passing the retreating Parker men as they moved slowly down the road to town. They swung their horses out of the way, blaspheming as the sorrel's flying hooves splattered them with mud.

As Shannon approached the edge of town, two pistol shots sounded somewhere ahead. He raced through the streets toward the jail, never doubting for an instant that it was there that the shots had been fired. It was now obvious that the incident at the cemetery had been orchestrated by Parker—he had sent the riders up to taunt the miners and start trouble. It had been a diversion, designed to keep Shannon busy long enough to give the rest of Parker's men time to assault the jail and try to spring Smith. And he had let it happen.

Furious with himself, he drove the mare headlong down the main street. As he pounded past the Lucky Lady he saw that Parker and Slade were standing on the walk in front of the saloon. Parker turned to watch him go by, and Shannon saw the expression of smug satisfaction on the man's face.

As Shannon approached the jail a man ran out of the door of the sheriff's office, then turned and fired his six-gun twice through the open doorway. Inside the jail a shotgun bellowed once more; Pop Bentley was putting up a fight.

The man in the street raised his six-gun to shoot again into the office. Shannon fired at him, not expecting to hit him from the back of a galloping horse but knowing it would distract his attention from the jail and perhaps prevent him from firing again at Bent-ley.

The gunman whirled as the bullet kicked up mud near his feet. His mouth dropped open in surprise; he uttered an oath and fired at the approaching lawman. The shot missed. The gunman fanned the hammer of the six-gun, but the weapon was empty. He cursed again, then turned and ran as fast as he could up the alley. Shannon got off one more shot at him as he passed the stable, but the man disappeared around the corner without breaking stride.

Shannon brought the mare skidding to a halt in a spray of mud right in front of the office. As he started to swing from the saddle, Pop Bentley came running out of the door.

"Clay!" he cried. "They're trying to bust Smith out through the cell window!"

Shannon regained the saddle and spurred the mare around the corner of the office to the side where the cells were located. Two riders were there, their horses straining against the ropes tied to the window bars of Smith's cell. At that moment the entire iron frame of the window came hurtling out of the wall, bars and all, accompanied by a cloud of mortar dust. Part of the jail wall also gave way as the window frame was pulled out of it, and broken bricks cascaded into the alley. The two horsemen turned in astonishment as the sorrel charged around the corner of the building. They immediately spurred their mounts down the side of the jail and around the back of the stable, the barred window frame bouncing crazily along behind them at the ends of the ropes.

As Shannon reached the gaping cell window, the prisoner, Smith, was just throwing his leg over the wrecked sill to climb out. He dropped hastily to the ground only to find himself looking into the muzzle of Shannon's Colt as the deputy brought the mare to a sliding stop beside the startled prisoner.

"Not this time, Smith," Shannon said, trying to keep the excited mare steady long enough to dismount. "Hold it right there."

Smith looked wildly around, gathering himself to make a break for it.

"Don't try it," Shannon said, swinging to the ground without taking his gun off Smith. "I'll drill you before you get ten feet." He motioned toward the street. "Put your hands above your head and walk toward the front of the jail. And no tricks—I'll be right behind you."

He marched the crestfallen prisoner around to the front of the building. After tying the sorrel to the hitch rail he herded the man through the front door into the office.

"Okay, Pop," he said. "Lock him in the other cell." He reached into the desk drawer and tossed Bentley a pair of handcuffs. "Here," he said. "Cuff him to the bars—that'll slow him down in case he gets any more funny ideas."

"His pals get away?" said Bentley.

"Yes," said Shannon regretfully. "I couldn't go after them because I had to keep this jailbird from flying away."

He watched as Bentley handcuffed Smith to the bars of the undamaged cell.

"Who were your friends, Smith?" he said. Smith leered at him.

"Never saw 'em before," he said.

"Of course not," said Shannon. "You know any of 'em, Pop?"

"Seen 'em around," Bentley replied. "Don't know their names, though."

"Well," Shannon said, "whoever they were, you can bet they had 'Ace Parker' branded on their backsides." He walked back into the office and slumped disgustedly in the chair behind the desk.

"Another chance wasted," he growled. "Trying to pin anything on Parker is like trying to catch the wind. Every time I think I've got something on him I grab an armful of air."

"At least we still got Smith," said Pop. "They didn't get him out."

"Not this time, anyway," Shannon said. "But it was close."

He kicked the desk drawer shut with his foot, then

leaned his elbows on the desktop and put his head in his hands. The thing was getting out of hand; there were too many against him, and everything he did seemed to come to nothing. He should have stayed at the jail that morning. But then, he reminded himself, if he had stayed in town there probably would have had a pitched battle at the cemetery, and people would have been killed. He had known he was taking a risk leaving the jail to go up to Boot Hill—it didn't take a genius to figure that Parker might try to break Smith out while he was absent. But he had known also that the decision to bury Spence on Boot Hill instead of carrying him back to the mining camp had created a ready-made recipe for trouble. He couldn't have been both places at once.

He stood up and walked to the window. This time it had worked out all right. As Pop said, they still had their prisoner. But what about next time? He might not be so fortunate again.

He needed help. Another pair of eyes, another gun. Somebody to cover his back. But even if he sent word to the county seat that very afternoon, it would be many days before help could arrive—even assuming Sheriff Hollister had anyone he could send.

And there was something else, too, a matter of professional pride. His reputation as a lawman was at stake. He had walked into this job with his eyes open. Hollister had warned him what to expect, that he would be on his own. If he failed here, he would be finished as a lawman, at least in this part of the country. No, he had to deal with it himself.

Or die trying.

Chapter Nine

A half-hour later he knocked at the door of Pedro Rodriguez' adobe. Rodriguez himself opened the door even as Shannon was knocking—he had obviously been keeping a lookout.

"Any problem here last night, Pete?"

"No, none. Come in, *amigo*. Maria just made some coffee. You had some trouble at the jail this morning, I think."

"You could say that," Shannon said wryly.

Inside the house, he accepted the coffee cup and sipped at the hot liquid. He told Rodriguez about the attempt to extract Smith from his cell.

"Maria told me about it," Rodriguez said. "I was up at the freight yard when it happened. We draw our pay on Fridays, and I went to get my money. I am sorry I missed the fun."

"Some fun," Shannon said glumly.

"You and Pop are all right? No one is hurt?" Rodriguez asked.

118

"No, nobody got hurt. We were lucky."

Shannon took another sip of coffee, trying to decide how to say what he had come to say.

"Look, Pete," he said finally, "there's something I need to talk to you about."

"Of course, *amigo*. What is it?"

"Well, it's just that things are getting a little rough around here, and I can't send up to the county seat for help. Even if they could spare somebody, I couldn't get anyone down here inside a week, and that's too long. Besides, I'm supposed to get the job done without bothering them. That's what they sent me for."

He hesitated, then reached into his pocket, pulled out a deputy's badge, and held it out to Rodriguez.

"I hate to ask you after you've already done so much for me," he said, "but the fact is I need somebody to cover my back for the next few days—somebody who knows what he's doing and can handle a gun if it comes to that. I was wondering how you'd feel about being a lawman again for a while, at least until I get this trouble with Parker settled. The pay's bad and the badge makes you a prime target for every would-be gunman who comes through town. Nobody in his right mind would take the job, especially right now. If you don't want to do it, I'll understand. You've got your family to think of."

Rodriguez took the badge gingerly from the other's

hand and stared at it for a moment. Then a smile spread slowly across his face.

"It would be like being young again," he said. "Those were great days in San Antonio. As for being a target, I guess I'm in *Señor* Parker's bad books after last night anyway. It would do little harm to make it— how do you say—official."

"Please think very carefully before you accept," Shannon said. "I don't want you to do anything that might put your family at risk. Parker's a swine. I don't think there's anything he wouldn't do."

"If we are successful," Rodriguez replied, "my children will have a better, safer town to grow up in. That is worth fighting for."

He pinned the star to his shirt.

"Let us begin," he said.

Shannon's first priority was to find some way to speak with Hilda Gibbs privately, away from the prying eyes and ears of Mrs. Williamson and Parker's other "associates." Knowing he dared not approach her himself in either the saloon or boardinghouse, he finally arranged with Pedro Rodriguez to have a young Mexican boy deliver a note to Gibbs at Mrs. Williamson's, asking her to meet Shannon that evening at a safe location.

"Don't give the note to anyone else, *chico*," Rodriguez cautioned the boy. "And tell *Señorita* Gibbs to destroy it as soon as she's read it. *Comprendes?*"

"*Sí, patrón,*" said the boy.

"You know what to say if someone asks you why you want to see the *Señorita?*" asked Shannon. They had coached the child carefully against just this eventuality.

"*Sí, patrón,*" the boy said again. "I know what you wish me to say." He hurried away up the street.

They waited uneasily in the office for the boy's return and Gibbs' answer. Ten minutes later their messenger slipped back through the office door. He looked upset.

"What did she say, *chico?*" asked Rodriguez.

"I'm sorry, *Señor,* she said she would not come."

Shannon swore under his breath.

"Did she tear up the note as we warned her to do?" he asked the boy.

"I don't know, *Señor.* She shouted at me and called me names, so I ran away."

"All right, Juan," Shannon said to the boy. "Thank you for your help. Here's two bits. Give it to your mother, and tell her she has a fine son."

"What next?" said Rodriguez, after the boy had gone.

"I don't know," said Shannon. "It looks like another dead end. The woman knows something about Watkins' death, but I hate to risk another contact with her;

I've already put her in danger. I just hope she got rid of that note before anybody else saw it."

Shannon ate lunch at Kathy Winters' café, then went to talk to the barber who had buried Watkins. He found the man in his shop, sitting slouched in his own barber chair and swigging green fluid out of a hair tonic bottle. The man was half drunk, and Shannon could get little useful information from him. Watkins had been brought to the barber shop dead, shot in the back, and the barber had piled the corpse into the coffin and buried it.

"Who paid for the burying?" Shannon asked.

"Nobody. Found a coupla dollars in the deputy's pocket. Want a drink?"

"No. Just a couple of dollars?"

"Yeah," said the man, looking suspiciously at Shannon. "You accusing me of robbing him or something?"

"No, just trying to find out what happened. Who carried the body up here?"

"The Doc and a couple of miners. I put him in a box and hauled him up to Boot Hill, just like I always do. That's all I know about it. Sure you won't have a drink?"

"Some other time."

Doctor Purcell confirmed that after Pedro Rodriguez had summoned him to the alley to examine Watkins, the doctor and two miners had carried Watkins' body to the barber's.

"Why?" Purcell asked. "Is it important?"

"No," said Shannon. "I just wondered who might have taken an interest."

"Not much of anybody," grunted Purcell. "Dead bodies aren't exactly a novelty around here."

"Even the bodies of deputy sheriffs?"

"No, that's the only one of those we've had. So far, that is."

Late that afternoon, Shannon returned to his office and sat down at the desk. The light of the setting sun streamed in through the open shutters, painting the dingy office blood red. Shannon lit the lamp, then unlocked the gun rack, took out one of the shotguns, and began to clean it.

He had been at this task for perhaps five minutes when he detected footfalls on the boardwalk outside the office. He quickly slid two shells into the chambers of the shotgun and silently closed the breech, then swung the muzzle of the weapon toward the office door just as it swung open. Nick Slade was standing in the doorway, watching him with cynical amusement.

"You're gettin' careless, Deputy," he said. "That could be fatal in your line of work."

Shannon put the shotgun on the desk and stood up.

"What do you want, Slade?" he said.

"Got a message for you."

"Which is?"

"Stay away from Hilda Gibbs."

"Why?"

"She don't want nuthin' to do with you."

"Did she say that?"

Slade reached into his pocket and pulled out a small piece of paper. It was the note Shannon had sent to Gibbs earlier in the day. Slade tossed it on the floor.

"Yeah," he said with a smirk, "she said it."

"You're sure it wasn't Ace Parker?"

"Just stay away from her, Shannon. You're messing in things that don't concern you."

"Murder always concerns me."

"Just stay away from her."

"All right, Slade, you can go back and tell Parker you delivered his message. Again."

Slade glowered at him.

"I'm through bringing you messages, Deputy," he said. "The next time I come, it won't be to talk."

The gunman wheeled and disappeared up the walk toward the Lucky Lady. Shannon stood in the door and watched him thoughtfully for a moment. The sun had now gone down, and there was a growing chill in the air.

* * *

The rest of the evening passed without incident. Rodriguez returned at suppertime and remained in the office with Shannon and Pop Bentley until midnight; then the deputy sent him home. Rodriguez went under protest, vowing to be back at dawn.

For two hours Shannon dozed fitfully on the lumpy bunk, waking at the slightest sound, then falling half-asleep again only to be jerked back to wakefulness by some small noise. In the jail, Pop Bentley and their prisoner slept soundly, while in the office Shannon waited for daylight. He kept thinking of Slade's most recent visit to the office. There was no mistaking the menace in the message—or in Slade's manner. Shannon was now certain that, sooner or later, he would have to deal with Parker's aide and personal killer.

Could he outdraw Slade if it came to that? He thought it possible but far from certain. Slade would be fast—his hand might well be quicker than Shannon's. But Shannon, with a lifetime of experience with guns and gunmen, had noted several things about Slade that might be important in a showdown. First of all, Slade's weapons were the long-barreled model Colts. A seven-and-a-half-inch barrel might look impressive to some, but Slade's guns would take longer to clear leather than Shannon's shorter-barreled Peacemaker. The difference would be minute, but it might be critical. In addition, like many gunmen who liked to look the part, Slade wore his guns too low. It would

take him a fraction of a second longer to draw and
cock his weapons because of that simple error. And
the black frock coat that, like Parker, Slade wore
would impede his draw. Would these things be enough
to give Shannon a chance? Perhaps—in a fair fight.
But would Slade stand up to him in a fair fight? Even
if he were faster than Slade, speed would be of little
use to him if he were to be attacked from an ambush,
as Watkins apparently had been. A quick draw is ir-
relevant to a man who has already been killed by a
bullet in the back.

Oppressed by these speculations, Shannon got up,
walked over to one of the windows, and opened the
shutter. He looked out at the shadowy street, and reminded himself that there were many dark alleys and
unlighted doorways in Whiskey Creek. Then he went
back to the bunk, lay down again, and tried once more
to sleep.

At just past two in the morning footsteps sounded
along the boardwalk, followed by a pounding on the
office door. In one smooth motion, Shannon rolled out
of bed, reached for the gunbelt that hung on a peg
beside the cot, and slipped the Colt out of its holster.

"Talk to me," said Shannon, cocking the six-gun.

"It's me, Sheriff, George Cook," said the voice.

Shannon unlocked the door and stood back, the
muzzle of the Colt centered on the door.

"It's open," he said. The knob turned slowly and the door swung back to reveal Mrs. Williamson's simian bouncer standing on the boardwalk holding an oil lantern.

"Well?" Shannon said, wondering if George had come to avenge his painful trip down Mrs. Williamson's stairs.

"Miz. Williamson sent me to get you. She says you better come up to her place right away."

"Why?"

"It's Angel."

"Angel?" said Shannon blankly.

"Yeah," said George. "You know—Hilda. She's hung herself."

Shannon pushed past the bouncer, hurrying up the walk. Several men who were standing outside the Lucky Lady stared at him without expression as he passed.

A small crowd had gathered on Mrs. Williamson's steps. He shoved his way through and hurried up the stairwell to the second floor. The door to Hilda Gibbs' room was open, and lamplight flooded into the hallway. Several men and women in various stages of undress were crowded around the doorway, but they drew aside as Shannon reached the top of the stairs.

Hilda's thin form lay sprawled upon the bed. Her eyes had bulged wide and her tongue protruded darkly through her dead lips. A worn rope was tied around her neck in a slipknot. The rope had been cut about twelve inches from the knot; Doctor Purcell was in the process of removing it as Shannon knelt by the bed.

"Hung herself from the lamp hook up there," Purcell said calmly. Shannon could smell the whiskey on his breath.

Shannon stood up and examined the rope looped over the lamp hook set into the ceiling. The hook looked flimsy, but it had been strong enough to support the weight of Hilda Gibbs' frail body. The dangling end of the rope had been cut; the other end was tied securely to one of the bedposts.

"You cut her down?" Shannon said to the doctor.

"Naw," said Purcell. "George and Mrs. W. did that before I got here."

Shannon examined the rope marks around the corpse's neck, then lifted up one of the dead woman's limp arms.

"Hasn't been dead long," said Purcell. "No signs of rigor mortis yet." He pulled a flask out of his coat and took a swig. "Not the first time one of these girls has decided to call it quits," he said indifferently. "Sometimes we get two or three suicides a week around here."

"It wasn't suicide," said Shannon grimly.

"Don't be a fool," said Purcell. "Anybody can see she hung herself."

"If she did," Shannon snapped, "she did it with her

hands tied behind her." He held up the dangling arm. A dark furrow was clearly visible around the circumference of the wrist. Purcell stared at it blankly.

"Wasn't anything around her wrists when I got here," he mumbled. "Maybe somebody tied her up some other time."

"No," said Shannon, easing the dead arm down to the corpse's side. "Those marks are obviously fresh. She was tied up while she was alive, and untied after she was dead. You ought to have seen that too, *Doctor*." He turned to face the onlookers crowded in the door.

"Any of you know how this happened?" he said.

There was a general muttering and shaking of heads. None of the suddenly nervous spectators would meet Shannon's eyes, and one by one they began backing out of the room.

"Thanks, folks," muttered Shannon, watching them go. He turned his attention back to the doctor. "What about you, Doc?" he said. "Any ideas about this?"

Purcell slipped his stethoscope back into his battered black bag.

"No," he said, "and I'm not gonna get any, either. If I were you, Deputy, I'd stay out of this."

"Not a chance. If this town had just had the backbone to stand up to Parker and his crowd a long time ago, a lot of dead people would still be alive."

"If you had let things alone, *she'd* still be alive,"

said Purcell, motioning toward the body. Shannon considered this for a moment, then nodded slowly.

"Well, I guess you're right about that," he said.

"Aw, don't take it so hard," said Purcell. "She was only a saloon girl. She didn't have much of a life."

"She was a human being," Shannon said, "and nobody deserves to die like that."

The doctor sighed and closed his bag.

"It's no use worrying about it, Deputy," he said quietly. "Your problem is, you take your job too seriously. You can't beat this town. It is what it is. Whiskey Creek is a wild animal, and you'll never tame it. You might as well give up and ride out of here while you still can."

"Not a chance," Shannon said, staring at Hilda Gibbs' dead face. "I'm going to bring the law to this town even if it kills me."

Purcell shrugged and took another drink from the flask.

"It just might do that, son," he murmured. But Shannon didn't hear him; he was already on his way out the door and down the stairs.

Shannon cornered Mrs. Williamson in the parlor off the front hall.

"Who found her?" he said.

"I did," said Mrs. Williamson in a flat voice.

"What time?"

"I dunno. Around one-thirty, I guess."

"Why did you go to her room at that hour?"

"One of her regulars came in here askin' for her."

"Who was that?"

Mrs. Williamson eyed him with contempt.

"I forget his name," she said.

"Try to remember."

"Sorry."

Shannon stared at her thoughtfully for a moment. Then he turned and deliberately kicked over a small table standing nearby. A vase and two picture frames went crashing to the floor.

"Hey!" the woman bellowed. "You can't—"

Shannon put his nose an inch from Mrs. Williamson's heavily painted face.

"Listen, *madam*," he hissed, "I'm sick of you and everyone else in this two-bit cathouse. I want to know what happened here tonight, and I want to know *now*. One more cute answer from you and I'm going to make kindling wood out of every piece of furniture in this room. Do you understand me?"

"George!" the woman bawled. "*George*!!!"

George appeared in the doorway, looking apprehensive.

"Come in, George," said Shannon smoothly. "I want a word with you, too."

I don't know nothin'," George said, backing away.

"None of us has anything to say to you, Deputy,"

Mrs. Williamson said. "So stop askin' questions. You want us to wind up like Angel?"

Shannon's anger faded.

"No," he said. "No, I don't."

"Then just go away and leave us alone. You can't help Angel now."

"I can try," said Shannon bitterly. "I owe her that much."

He pushed his way past George and went back up the stairs.

One by one, Shannon questioned the others in the building. He was not surprised to find that no one had seen anything, no one had heard anything, and no one knew anything. Finally he gave up in disgust and went back into Hilda Gibbs' room. The body had been removed, but the cord still dangled from the lamp hook in the ceiling. Shannon inspected the cord, but found nothing remarkable about it. Ordinary rope, ordinary knot. He went over the room inch by inch, hoping to find he knew not what. Something. Anything.

But there was nothing.

He took one final look around the room, then walked out.

He started down the street toward the sheriff's office. The night was cold, and he shivered a little in his thin shirt.

He had gone scarcely a dozen steps past the Lucky Lady when the muzzle blast of a shotgun erupted from the shadows of a doorway across the street. Buckshot whirred past him, and he threw himself down onto the walkway, clawing for his Colt. Horrid images of another night, another town, another shotgun filled his mind. He rolled off the walk into the dust of the street, sheltering behind a wooden horse trough there. The shotgun boomed again, and lead shot splintered the boards of the trough and the walk behind him. Then someone was running away up the street, past the Lucky Lady saloon, a shadowy form just visible in the starlight.

Shannon scrambled to his feet and gave chase. His saw that a hundred yards beyond the Lucky Lady his quarry had turned into an alley between the Whiskey Creek Hotel and the general store. Shannon plunged blindly into the alley after him, gasping for breath after the uphill run. He started down the narrow passage, hugging the wall of the hotel. In the shadows ahead he could just make out the form of his assailant, still running down the alley. Knowing he could not keep the man in sight much longer in the darkness, Shannon called to him to stop, not expecting him to do so. But indeed the gunman did stop; he halted, whirled, and raised the shotgun, pointing its muzzle directly at the oncoming lawman. The sound of the shotgun's hammers being cocked was clear and distinct in the cold air. Shannon fired twice; his hand was unsteady and the shots missed, but the roar of the Colt caused the attacker to flinch just as he pulled the shotgun's triggers, and the twin charges of buckshot went well over Shannon's head.

Cursing, the bushwhacker turned again and ran on down the alley. At the end of the hotel building he turned left, and Shannon heard a door slam. Almost certainly the man had run into the hotel through the back door. Shannon wheeled and raced back to the street, reloading his six-gun. He jerked open the front door of the hotel and charged into the lobby. The desk clerk was standing by the front window, wide-eyed.

"Where is he?" Shannon barked.

"N-nobody come through here," the desk clerk said nervously. "Heard somebody runnin' up the back stairs a minute ago, though."

Shannon strode rapidly to the lobby stairway and started up.

Pedro Rodriguez came through the front door behind him. Rodriguez was in his nightshirt, but he was wearing his gunbelt and his shotgun was clutched in his hands.

"What's going on, *amigo*?" he said.

"Somebody's using me for target practice again," Shannon replied. "He may be upstairs. Lend me the shotgun, will you?"

"Gladly," said Rodriguez, handing it over. "How else can I help?"

"Go around back and watch the rear door. If I flush him out upstairs, he may try to get out of the building the way he came in."

"*Bueno,*" said Rodriguez. "Take care, *compadre.*" He drew his revolver and hurried out the door.

Shannon climbed the stairs cautiously, the shotgun held at the ready. The wooden steps creaked beneath his feet as he ascended, and he cursed them silently. The second floor was dark, and Shannon braced himself. Somewhere above him, death was lurking. Suddenly, a dark form rose up over the railing at the top of the stairs and fired at him. Anticipating this, Shannon had already gone into a crouch, and again the buckshot slapped harmlessly past him.

Anger—anger mixed with fear—overwhelmed Shannon. He charged up the stairs, screaming curses at the top of his voice. His half-seen attacker bolted down the upper hallway toward the rear of the building. The man reached the end of the hallway and whirled, silhouetted against an uncurtained window.

"Drop it!" Shannon roared, leveling Rodriguez' shotgun at the man's midsection. "Drop it or you're a dead man!"

The man raised his weapon to fire again. Shannon pulled both triggers.

The double flash illuminated the entire hallway; in its light Shannon saw both charges of shot strike the gunman full in the chest. The impact propelled the man against the closed window; the sash splintered outward, and shards of shattered glass accompanied the body through the window and into the alley below.

Shannon stuck his head through the smashed window frame and looked down. The gunman lay sprawled in the dirt of the alley. Rodriguez was crouching over him, six-gun in his hand.

"He's dead," he said after a moment. "*Madre de Dios*, a shotgun makes a mess. But what about you? Are you hurt?"

"No," Shannon said. "Fortunately, he was a lousy shot. Wait there—I'll be right down."

He started down the back stairs. His hands were shaking so badly that he nearly dropped the empty shotgun twice on the way down.

The usual crowd was assembling around the body in the alley.

"Give me a light, here," Shannon said. The desk clerk came out of the back door with an oil lamp. Shannon inspected the dead man, trying not to look at the gaping hole in the corpse's chest. A ghastly feeling of *déjà vu* engulfed him. Another alley, another corpse. More blood. More death. Whiskey Creek seemed full of all of that. He looked again at the dreadful wounds, and felt bile rising in his throat.

"Anybody recognize him?" he said. No one answered.

They searched the gunman's pockets. There was no identification, but in one pants pocket they found a shiny fifty-dollar gold piece.

"Looks like he was just a drifter," said Rodriguez. "Ragged clothes, thin face, patched boots. Not the sort of man to have a fifty-dollar gold piece in his pocket."

"No," said Shannon. "I wonder who gave the money to him. And why."

"I think," said Rodriguez, "we can make a very good guess about that."

Someone had summoned the doctor, who soon appeared with his little black bag and his shirttails flapping. He snorted derisively when he saw Shannon.

"This is getting ridiculous, Deputy," he said. "I thought I'd seen the last of you for one night." He bent over the body.

"Dead," he mumbled.

"You amaze me," said Shannon.

"Think this is the one who killed the Gibbs woman?" said the doctor, standing up and reaching for his flask.

"I don't know, Doc," said Shannon, "but he certainly tried to kill me."

He turned to the onlookers.

"Go back to bed," he told them. "Show's over for tonight."

As the crowd dispersed, Shannon handed the empty shotgun back to Rodriguez.

"Thanks, Pete," he said. "I owe you another one."

"It was nothing," said Rodriguez. "Is there anything else to be done?"

"No," said Shannon, "not at the moment, anyway. I'm going back to the office. I'm tired of killing people in alleys, and I've seen enough death for one night. You go on home. I'll talk to you tomorrow."

"Good night, *amigo*. I'm glad you're all right."

"What makes you think I'm all right?" said Shannon, looking at his trembling hands.

Shannon left the hotel and walked unsteadily back down along the boardwalk, descending the hill toward his office. As he passed the Lucky Lady he glanced in through the swinging doors. Despite the hour, the bar was crowded, the tables busy. Whiskey Creek never slept—or at least the Lucky Lady never did. It was always awake, waiting.

Anger boiled up in Shannon, and he turned and started to push through the swinging doors to confront the drunken mob in the saloon, to ask if anyone there knew anything about Hilda Gibbs' murder or the attempt to kill him from ambush. But even as he touched the doors he checked himself and backed away from them. It was pointless to go inside. No one would talk.

As usual, there was no evidence. He would just be making a fool of himself—again.

Shannon found himself flooded with a powerful loathing for the Lucky Lady Saloon. To his tired mind it seemed that this garish structure was like some sleepless, malevolent beast, constantly vomiting its corruption and depravity out into the streets of Whiskey Creek, poisoning all it touched.

But that's foolish, he told himself. *I must be losing my grip. Buildings aren't corrupt or depraved, only the people in them. You can't hate a building.*

Yet even as he formed the thought, he realized he was wrong. He *did* hate the Lucky Lady Saloon, and all that it stood for.

"Someday I'll come for you," he whispered to the Lucky Lady. *"Someday I'll come for you—with or without the law."*

Shannon reentered the sheriff's office and slammed the door viciously behind him. Pop Bentley came out of the jail, holding a cocked rifle in his hands.

"What's goin' on?" he said. "I heard shootin'. Didn't want to leave the jail, because I thought they might be settin' up another try for Smith. You okay?"

"Yes. Barely."

"What happened?"

"Somebody tried to ambush me."

"Who was it?"

"Don't know. Some saddle tramp, maybe. Nobody seems to know who he was."

"You get him?"

"I got him."

"Good for you. What about that woman up at Mrs. Williamson's, the one that hung herself?"

Shannon sat down heavily on the bunk.

"She didn't hang herself. Somebody did the job for her. Strung her up like a butchered hog."

"Tarnation. Who done it?"

Shannon stared blankly at him for a moment. He remembered Doctor Purcell's accusation.

"In a way," he said in a low voice, "I guess I did."

"You?"

"If I hadn't charged into Mrs. Williamson's and started asking questions. . . . I should have been more careful about approaching Hilda, but I didn't know there was any connection between her and Watkins until Mrs. Williamson let it slip." He shook his head in self-disgust. "I blundered in there like a blind bull. And then, to make it worse, I tried to talk to her again, and it backfired. I was stupid, and Hilda Gibbs paid the price."

Shannon leaned forward and put his face in his hands. Suddenly he was very, very tired. He rolled over on the bunk and pulled the blanket around his shoulders.

"I don't want to talk about it anymore now, Pop," he said. "See you in the morning."

"Okay, son," said Bentley, scratching his head. "But don't blame yourself too much about Angel. You wuz just doin' your job. You ain't responsible for all the meanness in the world. Somebody else put the rope around her neck, not you." He turned to go back into the jail. "Get some sleep," he said as he shuffled out of the room.

But sleep would not come to Shannon during that long night. As the final hours of darkness dragged past, he tossed restlessly on the bunk, turning the events of the past days over and over in his mind. There seemed little question that Parker's men had killed the old prospector he had found on the trail. In addition, he was now almost certain that Slade had killed Watkins, either because the deputy had refused to cooperate or because he and Parker had a falling-out of some sort. And chances were that Parker had ordered, or at least condoned, some or all of the other killings—including that of Kathy Winters' husband.

And now the Gibbs woman. The image of Hilda Gibbs' distorted, ashen face haunted him mercilessly in the darkness. Undoubtedly she had seen the Watkins killing from her window, and because Shannon had talked to her about it, Parker had ordered her killed too. And as for the ambush on the street, as Rodriguez had said, it was not hard to guess where the fifty-dollar gold piece in the would-be assassin's pocket had come from.

But what proof did he have of any of it? Shannon was well aware that even under the rough-and-ready system of justice that prevailed in the region, he did not yet have enough evidence to obtain a conviction against Parker or Slade or any of Parker's men. Any smart defense lawyer would tear his case to shreds. But if he waited for better evidence, how many more people would die in the meantime? And if he waited too long, might not he himself be one of them? He had no illusions—Parker and Slade had already tried to kill him at least twice, perhaps three times. They would come after him again, sooner or later. Waiting would gain him nothing. He had held his hand too long already. It was time to take action.

He must have legal proof or act without it. He must satisfy the law—*or make his own.*

In the hour before dawn, he reached his decision.

The sky was just beginning to lighten on the eastern horizon when Pedro Rodriguez knocked quietly on the office door. Wearily, Shannon let him in.

"Glad to see you, Pete," he said—and meant it. Rodriguez sat down at the desk and leaned his chair back against the wall, his shotgun across his knees.

"I will stand guard," he said simply.

Shannon went back to the bunk, lay down upon it, and slept.

Chapter Ten

Shortly after nine o'clock, Shannon, now wide awake, came out of the office and looked carefully up and down the street. He saw miners drifting into town by twos and threes; it was Saturday, the day when they traditionally came down from the camp to have a few drinks and blow off some steam. By evening all of the saloons would be going full blast, and most of the miners would be roaring drunk. One way or another, Shannon reflected, it was going to be a busy day.

Leaving Rodriguez and Bentley to guard the jail, he stepped into the street and walked across to the restaurant. There were several customers in the dining room, so he drew Kathy Winters into the kitchen and closed the door. She listened wide-eyed as he told her about the events of the night.

When he had finished his account, Kathy shuddered and shook her head.

"This horrible town," she said. "Poor Angel."

She rested her hand on his arm.

"What happens now, Clay?" she said. "You look worried."

"I am worried. Parker isn't through by any means. There'll be more trouble soon, and when it happens I don't want you to get hurt."

"You think Parker will try something today?"

"Maybe, unless I do something first. The point is, I'd feel a lot better if you were somewhere else besides here. Can you go somewhere, visit someone in another part of town at least, until things calm down?"

She brushed a stray wisp of hair from her forehead and looked at him solemnly.

"I could," she said, "but I won't."

"Kathy . . ."

"No, Clay. I'm not going to run away. This is my place, and neither Parker nor anybody else is going to run me out of it. And I'm certainly not going to go sit in somebody's parlor on the other side of town, drinking coffee and wondering if you're in trouble, or hurt, or. . . ." She paused, biting her lip. "Anyway, I'm staying."

"All right," he sighed. "But please stay inside the restaurant today. Don't come to the office."

"Will I see you later?"

"I'll come over if I can. I may be pretty busy, though, so don't take it personally if I don't turn up."

"I understand," she said. She tried to smile, but

there was fear in her eyes. Shannon touched her hand and then turned to go.

"Good luck, Clay," she said. "Be careful."

He went out the door.

"Please, *please* be careful," she whispered to the empty kitchen.

When Shannon walked into his office, he found John Talbert and a half-dozen other miners crowded into the room. Pete Rodriguez was leaning against the wall near one of the windows, keeping watch through the half-opened shutters.

"These gentlemen wish to speak with you," he said. "They asked to be allowed to wait."

"Good morning, Mr. Talbert," Shannon said. "What can I do for you?"

Talbert looked uncomfortable.

"We heard Parker tired to bust Sam Spence's killer out of here," he said.

"That's right," Shannon replied. "They tried, but it didn't work. He's still here, under arrest and in a cell."

"They might try again," Talbert said. "What are you gonna do about that?"

"In a day or so, when I can, I'll take him up to the county seat. He'll be held in jail there until his trial."

"You think you'll get there alive? Parker's men will drygulch you before you get a mile out of town."

"They might try."

"Some of the people up at the camp are pretty hot about Spence's killing and the trouble at the cemetery," Talbert said. "A lot of the miners are coming into town today. There'll be a lot of whiskey and a lot of talk. A few of the boys are saying we ought to go right into the Lucky Lady and run Parker and his trash out of town. There's also some talk about taking Spence's killer out of the jail and stringing him up."

Shannon's face became hard.

"Now listen to me—all of you. Everybody can talk all they want to, but nobody's taking my prisoner out of here and nobody's going to clean out the Lucky Lady—nobody except me. This is my job, and I want you to leave me alone so I can do it. I've got enough on my hands right now without having to fight you people too."

He stepped closer to Talbert and looked him squarely in the eye.

"Talbert," he said, "you once asked me how you could help me. Now I'll tell you how. First, I want your word that you will do your best to prevent any of the miners from starting any trouble in the Lucky Lady today—for any reason. It would interfere with my plans. Next, I want your word that there won't be any miners coming around this office trying to hold a necktie party. Leave this to me, do you understand? *Leave it to me*. All right?"

Talbert scowled and looked at the others.

"I can't speak for all of the miners," he said slowly. "I ain't their boss or anything. What do you say, boys? Do you think we can get the others to play it the Sheriff's way?"

Grudgingly the others nodded their agreement.

"Okay," Talbert said, "we'll try. I can't promise nothin', but we'll do our best." He looked keenly at the deputy. "You say you got plans. What're you gonna do?"

Shannon grinned. "I'm going to clip Parker's wings a bit," he said.

"How you gonna do that?" Talbert said doubtfully.

"If you're around the Lucky Lady in about an hour, you'll see."

"When I see it, I'll believe it," Talbert said. The miners shuffled out, talking in low tones among themselves.

Rodriguez closed the door behind them and shook his head.

"Maybe you should have let them loose on Parker," he said. "They can fight pretty well, those miners."

"Slade and the rest of Parker's crew would cut them down before they got three feet inside the door," Shannon said. "The miners are tough enough in a Saturday night brawl, but they wouldn't have a prayer against professional gunslingers like Slade and Parker's other hired killers."

He laughed.

"That's what we get paid for, Pete," he said. "Us lawmen. Sixty dollars a month, rain or shine. If we live long enough to collect it."

"I think," said Rodriguez, "I should have stayed in San Antonio."

The clock on the wall was striking noon when Shannon came out of the office. Rodriguez followed him out the door.

"Remember," Shannon said to him, "all I want you to do is cover my back. Stay behind me, out of the line of fire. I'm hoping there'll be no shooting, but if there is I don't want those kids of yours to be orphans."

Rodriguez chuckled but said nothing.

The town was crowded with miners now, and shouts and laughter filled the street. As Shannon started toward the Lucky Lady he saw that a large group of miners had gathered outside the saloon's front door. One of them was Talbert. They watched him coming up the walk.

Shannon noted their presence with satisfaction. He had counted on Talbert and the rest talking loud enough to bring a curious crowd to the Lucky Lady. With luck, the saloon would be full of miners—and his life might depend on that simple fact. With so many witnesses present, Parker and Slade might be unwilling to start any gunplay. In that case he might just get away with what he was about to do.

He stopped outside the saloon and addressed Talbert and the rest.

"Don't forget, boys," he said, "keep out of this. Let me handle it." He looked over and saw that Rodriguez, following his orders, had taken up a position in a doorway across the street from the saloon. Rodriguez stood easily, his thumbs hooked in his gunbelt, but he looked worried. Almost as worried as I am, Shannon said to himself.

He pushed through the swinging doors and looked around. He had guessed right—the Lucky Lady was crowded with miners. The bar was packed three—deep and the gaming tables were surrounded. Heads turned as he came in, and men nudged each other and pointed at him. Gradually the noise in the room died away as one by one the room's occupants turned to stare.

Parker came out of the back room and pushed through the crowd. Inevitably, Slade was just behind him. Parker stopped a few feet away, one thumb tucked into his vest, the other hand holding his cigar.

"Well, Mr. Tin Star," Parker said, "you got a nerve coming in here like this. You already put one of my boys in your jail. What do you want now?"

A dead silence had fallen upon the room. When Shannon spoke his words, though softly he could be heard by everyone present.

"Mr. Parker," he said, "I'm closing your saloon."

Parker gaped at him.

"You're *loco*," he said. "You can't do that."

"I can, and I am," Shannon said. "You're running crooked gambling games. You're also harboring a lot of undesirable characters here—gunslingers and the like. And I've found stolen property in the possession of one of your employees, the late Mr. Ziebart. In short, you're breaking the law here, Mr. Parker, and that makes this establishment a public nuisance. I have the legal authority to close it down, and that's what I'm doing."

Parker was staring at him in total disbelief. His mouth was opening and closing silently. He looked like a fish out of water.

"You *are loco*," he gasped. "I run this town, and nobody tells me what to do. Nobody."

"Enough talk," said Shannon. "This place is out of business. The bar and the gaming tables are closed as of right now. No more liquor is to be sold, no more gambling allowed. All customers are to leave immediately. I'll give you until six o'clock tonight to pay off your employees and remove your personal property from the premises. By six o'clock I want everybody out of here and the doors padlocked. Padlocked, Mr. Parker. If I find anyone still here at six o'clock they'll be placed under arrest and taken to jail, and your property will be confiscated. Do you have any questions?"

Slade moved up beside Parker. His hands were at his sides, close to the handles of his six-guns, and he looked eagerly at Shannon.

"Ace, let me kill him right now," he said in a low voice. Shannon tensed, knowing this was the decisive moment. Parker might back down, or he might fight. It could go either way.

"Come on, Ace, let me gun him," Slade insisted.

Parker hesitated. Shannon held us breath. Whether he lived or died might depend upon Parker's next words.

"No, hold it," said Parker angrily. "It's no good." He looked around him. "Too many people. We'll wait." He glared at Shannon with undisguised hatred. "All right, Deputy," he snarled, "you win—for now."

He turned to face the room.

"Okay boys," he called. "Bar's closed. Sorry. Cash in your chips. We're closin' the place up for today." He glowered at Shannon again, still chewing angrily on his cigar.

"Satisfied?" he said, his eyes smouldering.

Shannon did not reply. He waited calmly as the miners finished their drinks and began filing out of the saloon.

"Hey Sheriff," said one, "you ain't gonna close *all* the saloons in town are you?"

Shannon laughed and shook his head.

"No indeed. Plenty of other places left. Have fun, boys."

Once outside the saloon, some of the miners began drifting away toward the other establishments in town. Many remained congregated outside the door of the Lucky Lady, peering in. Shannon guessed they were waiting to see if he was going to get out of the saloon alive.

"Ace . . ." Slade said again.

"Forget it," Parker said. "Just let it go for now. This ain't our only place—we ain't gonna go broke. We'll deal with this law dog later."

"Remember," Shannon said to Parker when the room had been cleared, "the doors are to be locked by six o'clock tonight, without fail. And don't get any fancy ideas about trying to reopen once I'm out of sight. If you do that, I'll know about it. The Lucky Lady is closed, and it had better stay that way."

He reached into his shirt and extracted the fifty-dollar gold piece he had found on the dead man behind the hotel.

"Here," he said, tossing the coin onto the floor at Parker's feet. "I believe this is yours. The next time I find it in some sneaking bushwhacker's pocket, I'll shove it down your filthy throat."

He wheeled and walked out the door through the gaping crowd of miners. Pedro Rodriguez, waiting tensely across the street, grinned broadly as he emerged from the saloon and turned down the hill toward the office. Rodriguez moved down the walk on the opposite side of the street, keeping abreast of Shannon and watching the saloon door until Shannon had reached the office safely. Then he crossed the street and followed him inside.

"*Santa María!*" Rodriguez said. "I never thought you'd get away with it!"

Shannon sat down at the desk to conceal the sudden weakness in his knees. He wondered if anyone had noticed that his hands were trembling.

"We haven't gotten away with it yet," he said. "I surprised them just now, caught them off balance in front of a lot of witnesses. But Parker won't give up so easily. The next time may be different. One thing we can count on—whether it's today, tomorrow, or a week from now—he'll try something."

"*Sí,*" Rodriguez snorted, "something like shooting you in the back when you go up there tonight at six o'clock."

Shannon nodded. It would be the logical time for Parker—or Slade—to make a play. It would be dark, and the miners wouldn't be there to act as an unknowing shield for him. Parker and Slade could wait for him, shoot him down, and then have the saloon running full blast again by seven o'clock.

He waited unhappily through the long afternoon, the

tension growing in him as the hands of the clock moved slowly toward six P.M.

But nothing happened. He came up the street at five minutes past six to find the Lucky Lady dark, the doors padlocked, and no one in sight. The worst moment was when he had to go into the alley past the spot where Watkins had died to check the rear door of the saloon. But it too was locked, and nothing stirred in the alley except a stray cat which was foraging in a garbage pail two doors away. Shannon came out of the alley sweating, feeling that he had aged ten years in the past ten minutes. At the Wagon Wheel Saloon a block away a piano was playing and miners were going in and out. Clearly they had found entertainment enough in Whiskey Creek's other saloons.

Rodriguez, who had been covering him while he was in the alley, fell in step beside him as they headed back toward the office.

"No trouble back there?" he said.

"I almost drew on a cat," Shannon said ruefully, "but that's all."

They went into the office, where Pop Bentley was sitting with a shotgun across his knees.

"Didn't really expect to see you fellas again," Bentley said cheerfully. "It's hard to believe Parker and his pals are gonna give up without a fight."

"They won't," said Shannon. "We're all going to have to sleep with one eye open from now on. Especially me."

Chapter Eleven

Contrary to Shannon's expectations, the night passed without incident, as did the next day—and the next. The Lucky Lady remained dark and empty, and of Parker and his men there was no sign. Parker owned a fancy bordello on the other side of town, and word reached Shannon that he was holed up there, keeping out of sight.

Pop Bentley announced that he had seen two of Parker's men riding out of town at a fast trot on Sunday morning. They took the stage road to the north and were not seen returning. Shannon wondered whether they were pulling out or were on some errand for Parker, but he had no way of knowing the answer.

Late Sunday night when no one was on the street, Shannon brought Smith out of the cell, handcuffed him, and put him on a rented horse. Rodriguez would escort the prisoner up to the county seat and deposit him in the jail there. Shannon had delayed their departure until long after dark in order to avoid observation.

"Watch your back," Shannon said to Rodriguez as

the latter mounted up. "They're not likely to have anybody posted on the road this time of night, but the minute they hear that Smith isn't still in the jail they'll probably send somebody to try to catch up with you."

He handed Rodriguez his own Winchester.

"If I see anybody starting out after you," he said, "I'll try to stop them, but I may not see them leave. Be ready."

"Don't worry," Rodriguez replied, caressing his shotgun. "I'll be ready."

Smith snickered loudly.

"One other thing, Pete," Shannon said, looking directly at Smith. "If this back-shooting skunk gives you any trouble—any trouble at all—*kill him.*"

"It will be a pleasure," said Rodriguez. He winked at Shannon. "Perhaps I will just gut-shoot him anyway and leave him by the trail to die. It would save me a long ride, no?"

Smith's sneer disappeared abruptly. He stared at them, his eyes suddenly frightened.

Rodriguez waved a farewell to Shannon and then motioned to Smith to lead out. The sound of their horses faded quickly into the night.

Shannon watched them go with some apprehension. He had not wanted to send Rodriguez off with Smith, but he had to get the prisoner out of Whiskey Creek. As long as he was in the town's jail he would be a lightning rod for trouble. Even if Parker didn't try

again to get him out, the miners might come for him
with a rope, and then Shannon would be forced to
defend his prisoner against men whom he did not want
to have to hurt or kill. Yet he hated to put Rodriguez
into danger by sending him off alone with the prisoner
on the long road to the county seat. He would rather
have gone himself, but he dared not. If he left town,
Parker would take immediate advantage of it, and
Rodriguez and Pop Bentley would be left to face them
alone. No, he had to stay and keep the lid on for as
long as he could.

Besides, he told himself, the way things were going,
Rodriguez might be safer on the trail than he would
be in town. Especially if things in Whiskey Creek
were about to boil over.

He went back into the office, sat down at his desk,
and began the vigil.

Rodriguez came back four days later, tired but triumphant. There had been no trouble on the trail, he
reported, and Smith was now locked in the county jail
awaiting the arrival of the circuit judge. Rodriguez'
red-rimmed eyes glinted with pride as he told how he
had ridden doggedly behind Smith, not sleeping and
stopping only to rest the horses briefly until he had
reached the county seat and turned Smith safely over
to Sheriff Hollister. He had gotten three hours' sleep
on a cot in the county jail and then mounted up to

return to Whiskey Creek. And, he announced with obvious pride, before he had left the county seat Hollister had approved his appointment as deputy.

Shannon, greatly relieved to have Rodriguez back safely, told him to go home to his family, get some sleep, and come back to the office on Saturday when the miners would again be in town.

With all remaining quiet during that long week, Shannon spent much of his time with Kathy Winters. One afternoon they picnicked among the cottonwood trees outside of town, and after they had eaten they walked together along the river. When at last they sat down beneath one of the big cottonwoods to rest, Shannon leaned back against the trunk and looked out thoughtfully at the rippling water.

"This is nice," he said. "There haven't been many moments like this in my life. Certainly not in Whiskey Creek. It seems strange to find this sort of peacefulness in the middle of all the violence."

"Yes," Kathy murmured. "It *is* nice here, now, with you. If only we could somehow make the peacefulness last. Do you ever find yourself wishing that tomorrow would never come?"

"I guess most people wish that at one time or another," Shannon said. "But whether you want it to or not, tomorrow always does come. The trick is to be alive when it does."

"Don't say that. I'm afraid for you."

Shannon didn't answer. He picked up a pebble and threw it into the stream. They watched it sink out of sight.

"What will you do with them, Clay?" she said.

"Do with what?"

"The tomorrows. When all of this trouble is over, where will you go, and what will you do?"

"I don't know," he said. "I've learned it's not wise to plan too far ahead."

"You could go *now*, you know," she said in a small voice.

"Go?"

"Yes. Leave Whiskey Creek. Pull out. Go somewhere else. Do something else. Be something else. Open a store. Have grandchildren. Live to a ripe old age. Forget this awful town. You don't owe it anything. Certainly not your life."

Shannon looked at her, perplexed.

"I can't run. You know that."

She sighed.

"Yes, I know it. That's not the way you're made. You're a brave, foolish, stubborn man. You'll never run, no matter what the odds. And you'll never stop carrying the star, either, will you?"

"Probably not. I'm afraid I'm just not cut out for storekeeping."

"Well, no matter what, I suppose Whiskey Creek will still need a sheriff," she said glumly.

Shannon laughed.

"No doubt about that," he said. "There's always work for a lawman in a mining town."

He sobered, watching her face.

"What about you, Kathy? Are you planning to stay here? After we find your husband's killer, I mean."

"Perhaps. It depends."

"On what?"

"On whether there's anything to stay for. Or any-one."

"Oh," he said, a little taken aback. "Is there. Is there someone now?"

"I think so," she said. "In fact, I'm pretty sure there is."

She smiled at him—a little, secret, playful smile. Shannon had never experienced that sort of smile before. It occurred to him that the day had suddenly become very warm.

After that, Shannon ate all of his meals at the restaurant, and each evening after closing time he and Kathy Winters sat and talked in the empty dining room or in the shelter of the darkness outside the sheriff's office. By the end of the week, although they had not yet put it into words, they were both aware that in each other they had found something worth holding onto—something each of them desperately needed, something both of them wanted more than anything else on earth.

For that reason alone this might have been a good and memorable week for Clay Shannon, yet he was far from content. He knew with painful certainty that the tranquility of these days was a pleasant illusion, that his time with Kathy Winters might well be nearing an end, and that a showdown with Parker, however long delayed, must eventually come. As his feelings for Kathy deepened, he found himself thinking more and more about the future and wishing fervently that a further confrontation with the denizens of the Lucky Lady would not be necessary, that Parker and the rest would give it up and leave Whiskey Creek for other climes without demanding a final reckoning.

Yet even as he wished for it he recognized it as a foolish hope, and indeed a dangerous one. That sort of wishful thinking could get him killed. Angrily he told himself that he had fallen into the very trap he had sworn to avoid—he had allowed himself to become distracted from the job at hand.

There would be a showdown, perhaps a sudden and violent one, and he must be ready for it. To fail to face that grim fact, to allow himself to be lulled into complacency by the false calm of the passing days and his own wistful desire for peace, could—and would—be fatal. He cleaned and reloaded his firearms each day, and slept fitfully through each night.

Chapter Twelve

Saturday morning dawned bright and sunny. Shannon viewed the golden sunrise without enthusiasm—soon the miners would begin to drift into town for their weekly carouse. By evening there would be scores of drunken men roaming the streets of Whiskey Creek.

As the clock was striking eight, Pedro Rodriguez came into the office.

"Think there'll be any trouble today, *amigo*?" he said.

"I wish I knew," said Shannon. "We'd better stay awake, just in case."

At mid-morning John Talbert and two other miners came by the office.

"You hear the news, Sheriff?" said Talbert in a gloomy voice.

"What news?"

"Freight wagon just came in from the county seat. Driver says somebody busted Smith out of the county jail. Held the jailer at gunpoint and took him right out of the cell. Looks like it didn't do no good to send him up there after all."

Shannon felt the anger and frustration surging up within him. Once again one of Parker's men had escaped justice, and once again all of his own efforts had been brought to nothing.

"Anybody hurt in the break?" he said.

"Not as I heard. They think he's headed north, out of the territory."

Well, that's something, anyway, Shannon thought. *At least he's not coming back here to rejoin Parker. One less gun to worry about.*

But he was worried nonetheless. Was this jail break the last move Parker was going to make? Of course not. At most it was a sideshow. The main event was still to come.

Shortly after noon, he sent Rodriguez out to take a look around. The deputy came back an hour later to report that the miners were still coming in, that they were starting to get liquored up, and that he had seen several strangers in town.

"Strangers?" Shannon said. "What did they look like?"

"Hard men. Guns worn low. Might have been from up north, by their look. Dodge City, maybe, or the Dakotas."

"How many?"

"Four that I saw."

"All together?"

"*Si*, all together."

"What were they doing?"

"Just riding through, as far as I could tell. They went up the street and I didn't see them again."

"Any mining gear with them?" Shannon asked hopefully. New people were always drifting in to try their hands in the gold fields.

"No," Rodriguez said. "They didn't look like miners. Let me put it this way—if we had a bank in this town, I'd be worried about these men. They had that kind of a look."

"Well, I don't like it," Shannon said, "but there's not much we can do about it for the moment. I guess we'll find out soon enough if they've come to make trouble."

He stayed close to the office for the rest of the afternoon. About three o'clock he sent Rodriguez out to take one more turn around town and to look for the four strange riders. Rodriguez came back without having sighted them.

"Just the usual goings-on for a Saturday," he announced to Shannon. "A lot of miners in town, most of them getting pretty drunk. We'll have a few fights before the evening is over, I think."

"Nothing else?"

"No, *nada*."

"I just don't like it," Shannon said. "It's too quiet."

"The calm before the storm, you think?" Rodriguez asked.

"I hope not," said Shannon.

A little after five o'clock, Kathy Winters came into the office. She had on the same blue dress she had been wearing the night Shannon had first met her, and it made him catch his breath a little just to see her in it again.

She brought supper for Shannon and Rodriguez, and sat with them as they ate. As twilight fell, Shannon closed the shutters and lit the oil lamp. He tried to make conversation with Kathy and Rodriguez, but he could not. The tension was growing in him again. Some instinct, some sixth sense born of too many years of waiting for trouble in too many towns was warning him that all was not well. Kathy noticed his tenseness.

"What is it, Clay?" she asked.

He shrugged.

"I don't know. Nothing, maybe. I'm getting old, I guess. Too old for this job, anyway. You're right—I ought to take up storekeeping or something."

"Something like running a restaurant?" said Kathy hopefully.

"I can't cook," he said, looking at the clock.

At five minutes to six Pop Bentley came hurrying down the street and pounded urgently on the door.

"Clay!" he puffed as they let him into the office. "The Lucky Lady is all lighted up. People are goin' in there. I took a look through the door—the bar is open and the tables are runnin'. Parker's opened the place up again."

Shannon felt a tightening in his chest. He had known that eventually Parker would make his move. Apparently this was it.

"I knew this past week was too good to be true," Kathy Winters said. "Oh, Clay!"

"It had to happen," he said. "It was just a question of when."

Someone else was knocking on the door. It was the miner, John Talbert.

"Sheriff," he said hesitantly, "I didn't know if you'd heard, so I thought I'd better tell you. The Lucky Lady's open again. I was just in there."

Shannon nodded in acknowledgment.

"Thanks Mr. Talbert. I heard. Is Parker there?"

"Yeah, big as life. Looking like the cat who ate the canary, too."

"What about Slade?"

"He's there, too. It looked like Parker's whole gang was there."

"Okay, Mr. Talbert. I appreciate you coming to tell me this. Thanks."

After Talbert had gone, Shannon looked around at the others. When he spoke, his voice was tired.

"Pete," he said, looks like we've got some more work to do."

Rodriguez wordlessly drew his six-gun and checked the cylinder.

"What about me?" Pop Bentley said. "What can I do?"

"Just stand by here, Pop," Shannon said, picking up his hat. "If . . . when we get back, we may have some prisoners."

He turned to Kathy Winters.

"Go back to the restaurant, Kathy," he said. "Stay there, no matter what happens. I'll come as soon as I can."

"I'd rather wait here with Pop."

"No. There may be trouble . . ."

He stopped, listening. He had heard a board creak on the walk outside.

Rodriguez said "What. . . . ?"

"Down!" Shannon shouted.

The shutters of all three windows exploded inward, splintered by buckshot. Flying glass from the smashed windowpanes sliced across the office. Shannon swept the lamp from the desktop, sending it crashing into a corner. His revolver was already in his hand as he hurled himself at Kathy Winters, dragging her to the floor and covering her body with his own.

Shotgun barrels came thrusting through the windows. They roared again and again, and a storm of lead shot swept the room. There was no time to run, no place to hide; the muzzle flashes turned night into hideous day, and the noise was stupefying. Shannon twisted himself to fire his Colt, shooting blindly at the shadowy forms outside the windows. With his second shot one of the attackers yelped and fell back out of sight. To his left, Shannon heard a gasp of pain followed by the bark of a six-gun—Rodriguez had been hit, but he could still fire back.

Then another blast from the windows shook the walls of the room, and Kathy Winters screamed. Shannon, still trying to shield her from the gunfire, felt her body convulse beneath him and go limp.

"Kathy!" he shouted. "Kathy!" There was no response.

Half-mad with shock and rage, Shannon ducked beneath still another hail of buckshot and fired twice through the closed door, then leaped to open it. He realized that it was suicidal to go charging out into those shotguns, but he had to draw the attackers' fire away from Kathy and Pete and Pop. As he reached out desperately for the latch another flash and roar came from the far window, and something burned through the flesh of his calf, knocking him to the floor. He rolled over and sent his last two shots through the window.

Abruptly the shotgun barrels were withdrawn, and the sound of running feet echoed along the boardwalk—at least three men, possibly four, were hurrying away into the dark. The footsteps faded quickly and were gone.

A terrible stillness settled upon the night.

Heedless of the risk, Shannon leaped up from the floor. Getting his bearings in the darkness, he limped to the corner of the room and groped around frantically for the extinguished oil lamp. The glass chimney had shattered, but the lamp itself was intact. He fumbled for a match, struck it, and applied it to the wick. The lamp gleamed feebly. He whirled around and held it up so that it illuminated the rest of the office.

Pedro Rodriguez was on the floor by the bunk, trying to get up. The right side of his shirt was soaked with blood. Pop Bentley's body lay near the door, stiffening in death. Part of his head was missing. Shannon's stomach turned over as he saw what the shotguns had done to the old man who had befriended him.

He tore his eyes away and looked frantically around for Kathy. After a panic-stricken moment he saw her lying crumpled up behind the desk where he had pushed her. He put the lamp down on the corner of the desk and lifted her up, cradling her in his arms. Her eyes were closed, and rivulets of blood were coursing down her face. He touched her throat, feeling for a pulse, and in that moment he lived and died and lived again—the pulse was weak and irregular, but it was there.

People were running up to the office, crowding in the door with shouts of astonishment and alarm. Oblivious to the wound in his leg, Shannon picked Kathy up and placed her gently on the bunk. He turned and crouched beside the struggling Rodriguez, helping him to a sitting position against the wall. Someone had brought another lamp and was holding it over them.

"En nombre de Dios," Rodriguez said weakly. "I was right—I should have stayed in Texas." Shannon ripped away his shirt. Two buckshot had struck Rodriguez in the fleshy part of his right side, while another had bounced off a rib, leaving an ugly gash. The wounds were bloody but not fatal. He squeezed Rodriguez' shoulder and bent over Kathy again.

"Hold that lamp here!" he said. "Quickly!"

A slug had torn the scalp over her left ear but had not penetrated her skull. Carefully, tenderly, he wiped the blood from her cheek. She opened her eyes and stared blankly at him for a moment. Then recognition came into her face.

"You're alive!" she whispered.

"I'm alive," he said, joy flooding through him. "I'm fine. So are you. Just lie still." She shuddered and reached up to him, holding on to him for dear life as the silent sobs wracked her body. He smoothed her hair, talking to her, reassuring her. Presently the shock began to wear off, and she lay back in Shannon's arms.

"I'm all right now, Clay," she said. "Is . . . is everyone else safe?"

Shannon, thinking of Pop Bentley's mangled corpse and Rodriguez' bloody wounds, could say nothing.

The doctor came hurrying in. As usual he reeked of whiskey, but the carnage in the office seemed to sober him quickly, and he began to fuss over Kathy and Pedro Rodriguez. After a few moments' examination of each of them he turned and looked solemnly at Shannon with his rheumy eyes.

"They'll make it," he said. "The woman's just got a crease in her scalp. Painful but not serious. I'll have to dig the lead out of Pedro's side, though. What about you? Looks like you caught one in the leg."

"Never mind me," Shannon snapped. "Take care of *them*."

John Talbert pushed his way through the crowd into the office. His face paled as he looked around at the devastation.

"Wh-What happened?" he stammered. "Who was it?"

Shannon got slowly to his feet. "Parker," he said.

Another miner came running up to the door and shoved his way into the room.

"Sheriff!" he shouted. "I saw it all! There were four of them. You winged one—the others had to help him get away. They all ran into the Lucky Lady."

Shannon nodded. The fleeing footsteps had faded

off in that direction. He bent and picked up his six-gun from the floor, put it on, then limped over to the desk. Ignoring the pain in his leg, he took a box of cartridges from the desk and carefully reloaded the Colt, then returned it to the holster. From the bottom drawer he removed another .45, checked its cylinder, and stuck the second weapon in the left side of his waistband. Then he pulled a shotgun out of the wall rack, broke it open, and shoved two shells into the chambers. Snapping the gun shut, he slipped a handful of twelve-gauge shells into his pocket and turned toward the door.

"*Vaya con Dios, amigo*," Rodriguez gasped. "I'll be along as soon as this butcher gets through with me."

"Stay put, Pete. I'll do this alone."

Talbert put a hand on Shannon's arm.

"Wait a minute, Sheriff," he said. "There's four of them, and Slade, and the rest of Parker's hired guns too. You can't . . ."

He stopped, shocked by what he saw in Shannon's face. It was a mask of cold fury. The intensity of his expression sent a chill down Talbert's spine—the miner had never before seen such hatred in a man's eyes.

Shannon threw Talbert's hand off his arm.

"Get out of my way," he said. He pushed the miner aside and moved toward the door. The crowd parted before him as if by magic, and he was on the sidewalk, striding through the darkness toward the lighted door-way of the Lucky Lady. The crowd came running after him, yelping like a pack of hounds.

Chapter Thirteen

A dozen men were gathered in front of the Lucky Lady Saloon. They scattered like autumn leaves as Shannon approached. Only one man remained standing in the light from saloon doorway, facing the lawman as he came. It was Slade.

"That's far enough, Shannon," Slade snarled. "This time we finish it."

Without breaking stride, Shannon shifted the shotgun to his left hand. Seeing the motion, Slade went for his revolver. As expected, he was fast—very fast. Shannon's Colt was just out of its holster, still coming up, when Slade fired; the muzzle flash of his six-gun lit up the street.

But Slade had made a fatal mistake—he had forgotten that just being fast was not enough. The slug seared the skin of Shannon's left side and struck a miner running up the walk behind him. Slade had committed the one unpardonable sin for a gunfighter— he had missed.

174

The Colt bucked once against Shannon's hand; Nick Slade dropped his six-gun and staggered back, howling and clutching at his belly. Shannon fired again, spinning Slade around. The gunman shrieked a second time, then staggered to the edge of the boardwalk, turned, and fell spread eagled on his back in the street. His limbs twitched once and then he lay still, his eyes staring sightlessly at the night sky.

Shannon did not even pause to look at the dead gunfighter. Still in full stride, he shoved two fresh cartridges into his revolver and holstered it, then resumed his grip on the shotgun. As he reached the doorway of the Lucky Lady he lifted the shotgun and with its butt smashed the swinging doors aside, knocking one off its hinges. It clattered into the saloon and skidded across the floor. Shannon followed it through the doorway.

The Lucky Lady was crowded. Many of the men were miners, but Shannon spotted at least five of Parker's gunhands around the room. As Shannon came through the door the crowd scurried hastily away from the bar and the tables, pressing against the walls to get out of the way. Ace Parker was left standing alone in the middle of the room.

When Shannon spoke it was almost in a whisper, but there was no mistaking the deadly intensity in his voice.

"Where are they, Parker?" he said.

Parker stared at him in consternation. He had been expecting Slade to walk back through the door with the news that Shannon was dead. Now he realized that it was Slade who was dead, and he felt fear.

"Where's who?" he said, trying to bluff it out.

"Your four hired murderers, Parker. Where are they?"

"I don't know what you're—"

Shannon swung the muzzle of the shotgun around and fired both barrels point blank into the long mirror behind the bar. The mirror disintegrated in a cloud of flying glass. The broken pieces cascaded down onto the bar, sending the two bartenders scuttling frantically out of the way. Parker's mouth hung open in disbelief as he stared at the fragments of plate glass strewn across the floor.

"That mirror cost me a fortune!" he cried. "I had it shipped all the way out here from Chicago!"

Shannon broke open the shotgun and reloaded it.

"Let's try it again, Parker," he said, slamming the gun shut. "Where are they?"

"I tell you I don't know what you mean. All my boys are—"

Shannon raised the muzzle of the shotgun above his head and pulled the trigger. One of the three large oil lamps hanging from the ceiling beams came crashing down onto the floor of the saloon in a shower of oil and glass. The spreading pool of kerosene burst into flame, igniting the floorboards. They began to burn fiercely.

Parker lurched backwards to get away from the fire.

"Don't move, Parker," Shannon hissed. "One more step and I'll kill you where you stand. Now, answer me if you want to live. *Where are they?*"

Parker was sweating.

"I tell you I—."

The shotgun muzzle rose toward the ceiling again. The blast brought down a second oil lamp from the beams above. Shannon was already reloading the shotgun as the lamp hit the floor. Again fire leaped up, and now Parker found himself caught between two growing lakes of flame.

"Help!" he screamed, his voice high-pitched with terror. "Shaw! Sullivan! Manney!"

Three men came plunging through the curtained doorway at the back of the room. Each was carrying a shotgun. They could have killed Shannon easily, but they too had made a mistake—they were bunched together when they came through the door. As they brought their weapons up, Shannon fired both barrels. The heavy shot slammed all three gunmen backwards; their weapons went flying as their torn bodies crashed to the floor. Blood began to seep across the floorboards.

A fourth man came stumbling through the curtain,

waving empty hands at Shannon as the latter rammed two more shells into his shotgun.

"Don't shoot," the man screamed. "Don't shoot!"

Shannon saw that this man was already wounded—one shoulder and sleeve of his shirt were blood-soaked. The fourth assassin. Shannon raised the shotgun until its muzzles pointed squarely at the man's chest. The gunman panicked and went for his holster. Again Shannon fired both barrels, and the man's torso dissolved into bloody rags.

Parker was still standing in the middle of the floor, paralyzed with fear. Shannon reloaded the shotgun yet again and pointed it at the terrified saloonkeeper.

"Parker," he said, "who killed Watkins?"

"How do I know?" Parker sniveled. He looked frantically around the room at his remaining men. "Shoot him!" he wailed. "Kill him!"

"Not me," said one, looking at the mutilated corpses of the four dead men. "I don't want to die like that."

"Me neither," said two others in unison.

"If it's all the same to you, Sheriff," said a fourth man, "I'll just head for Montana right now."

"Me too," said the fifth. "Okay, Sheriff?"

Without waiting for a reply, all five of Parker's men bolted out the back door into the night. Shannon let them go.

Parker also started for the back door, but Shannon's voice was like a whiplash.

"One more step, Parker," he said, "and I'll cut you in half."

Parker stopped and whirled to face him.

"What do you *want* from me?" he howled. He pointed to the flames which were now eating into the floorboards and licking up toward the ceiling. "We gotta get out of here! The place is on fire!"

"Who killed Watkins?"

"I told you I don't—"

Shannon shot down the third lamp from the ceiling. It too began to burn.

"Who killed Grubbs?"

"Who's Grubbs?"

"The miner I found on the trail coming in."

"I don't know anything about—"

"Who killed Hilda Gibbs?"

"You mean Angel? I didn't have nothin' to do with—"

In one swift movement, Shannon shifted the shotgun into his left hand and drew his Colt. He leveled it at one of the oil lamps hanging on the wall and fired. Burning kerosene ran down the boards onto the floor.

The onlookers in the saloon, who had been frozen in their tracks to that point, suddenly began scrambling madly for the doors.

"You're crazy," cried Parker. "This place is going to go up like a tinderbox!"

"Who killed Mrs. Winters' husband?"

"I swear I don't—"

Shannon shot out another wall lamp. The burning oil set fire to the wall beneath it. Five separate fires were now spreading rapidly along the dry boards of the walls and floor, and the flames illuminated the saloon more brightly than the lamps ever had.

Slowly, deliberately, Shannon shot out three more lamps. Two burned immediately. The third crashed to the floor without igniting, but the kerosene ran along the floor and joined one of the other fires. The flames ran back along the trail of oil and climbed rapidly up the wall. Now only Shannon and Parker remained in the room; everyone else—miners, gamblers, bartenders, and saloon girls—had fled. Shannon could see some of them peering wide-eyed at him through the windows.

The smoke and heat were becoming intense. Parker was now almost encircled by flame.

"For God's sake, Shannon," he whimpered, "I got to move! The fire's too hot!"

"One more time, Parker. *Who killed Watkins?*"

"Slade did it!" Parker shrieked in despair.

"On your orders?"

"Yes, yes, on my orders. Now let me go! I'll do anything!"

"And the prospector, Joe Grubbs?"

"Slade and Ziebart. Now let me—"

"What about Mrs. Winters' husband?"

"Ziebart did it."

"And Hilda Gibbs?"

"She knew too much. Slade killed her!"

"On your orders."

"*Yes*! For the love of . . . You gotta let me move! I'm gettin' burned!"

"Time to go, *amigo*," said a voice behind Shannon. He turned slightly and saw Pedro Rodriguez standing just inside the door, a bandage wrapped around his bare chest and a six-gun in his hand. Behind him in the doorway was John Talbert with a shotgun. And beside Rodriguez stood Kathy Winters, the bloodstains still fresh and bright on her calico dress. She was holding a Winchester rifle. The hammer was cocked.

Shannon looked back at Parker, the killing fury slowly subsiding in him. For the first time he became fully aware of the swirling smoke and leaping flame. The room was lit up—portions of three walls were on fire and half of the floor was aflame. A burning beam came crashing down from the ceiling in a hail of sparks. The heat was almost unbearable.

"All right, Parker," he said. "Come on out of there. You're under arrest for murder. Walk in front of me into the street. If you try to run I'll kill you."

The saloonkeeper dodged around the flaming portions of the floor and lunged for the front door. Shannon saw that the tail of his frock coat was smoking.

Parker seemed intent only on escape, but as he hurried past Shannon he suddenly whirled and thrust out his right arm. A twin-barreled derringer come sliding like a snake out of a hideout sleeve rig and into his palm. He thumbed back the hammer of the derringer and raised its twin muzzles toward Shannon's face, filthy oaths spewing from his mouth.

Shannon shot him between the eyes, blowing the back of his head off. Ace Parker was dead even before his body tumbled backwards into the flames.

Shannon holstered the Colt and walked unhurriedly out the front door.

Chapter Fourteen

They stood in the street together—miners, towns-people, Talbert, Rodriguez, Kathy Winters, and Clay Shannon. They watched, silent and unmoving, as the Lucky Lady burned. Some of the townspeople were frantically emptying buckets of water onto the roofs of the adjacent buildings to keep them from being set afire by drifting sparks.

No one tried to put out the fire that was consuming the Lucky Lady. With each passing minute the flames climbed higher, and billows of smoke went swirling up toward the starlit sky.

"Did you hear it?" said Shannon.

"Hear what?" said Talbert.

"It screamed," Shannon said.

"What screamed? Is somebody still in there?"

"No. The Lucky Lady screamed."

Talbert stared at him.

"It's only the beams creaking as they burn," he said. "Buildings don't scream."

"I suppose you're right," said Shannon indifferently. A great peace was creeping over him. It was as if the leaping flames were lifting a terrible burden from his shoulders, and for a moment he would have sworn that he could feel some sort of evil presence fading away into the night sky.

I'm imagining things, he said to himself. *It's just an ugly yellow saloon burning down. That's all.*

Suddenly, he was very tired.

Soon the roof of the building came crashing down in flames, and shortly afterwards the walls collapsed inward to stoke the inferno. The dry wood burned quickly, consuming everything. Within half an hour the Lucky Lady Saloon was just a pile of glowing embers.

People were crowding around Shannon, slapping him on the back, offering him a drink, calling out good wishes. He stood patiently through it all, his arm around Kathy Winters, until the fire had died out and the crowd had begun to disperse. Finally, as if awakening from a bad dream, the two of them turned away from the smoking pyre.

Shannon thanked John Talbert for his help. They shook hands, and Talbert moved away up the street.

"I think," said Pedro Rodriguez, "it is time for me to go home. My wounds are honorable but they are becoming a little painful, and my family will be worried. Good night, *amigo*. Good night, *señora*."

"Good night Pete," Shannon said. "And thank you for everything. I'll never forget what you've done."

"God bless you, Pedro," Kathy Winters said.

Rodriguez waved a hand to them in salute and departed.

When he had gone, Shannon stood for a moment holding Kathy close to him in the darkness.

"I'm so thankful it's over, Clay," she whispered, "and that you're safe. I was so frightened when you were in there with those killers. I was afraid I'd lose you."

"I'm not so easy to lose," Shannon said, looking down at her. She laughed.

"Neither am I," she said softly.

They walked down the hill together, into the night.